Calling all valiant Astra Daim

THE ATLANTIS GRAIL COMPANION is here to guide you by means of Starlight through the expansive universe of *The Atlantis Grail*.

This is our first comprehensive reference book of all things TAG for superfans—that's all of you awesome readers and lovers of TAG! Published in ebook and handsome paper print editions (hardcover and paperback), it's a cornucopia of fun facts, explanations, in-depth expansions and revelations, including a full *Atlanteo* language glossary, cultural references, an exploration of Atlantean society, the military Fleet, foods of TAG, places, terms, definitions, maps, and even drawings and rough sketches the author made when writing the original four-book series! Plus, so much more, with tons of surprises, easter eggs, and some *new*, previously unpublished goodies just for *YOU*!

So, don't be shy, open this exciting collector volume and start exploring!

THE ATLANTIS GRAIL COMPANION is a part of The Atlantis Grail Superfan Extras series.

This book is a work of fiction. All characters, names, locations, and events portrayed in this book are fictional or used in an imaginary manner to entertain, and any resemblance to any real people, situations, or incidents is purely coincidental.

THE ATLANTIS GRAIL COMPANION
A Reference Guide to Things and Places for Fans of The Atlantis Grail
(The Atlantis Grail Superfan Extras Series)

Vera Nazarian

Cover Design Copyright © 2021 by Vera Nazarian
Cover image elements: "Spiral galaxy in deep space — Photo" by sakkmesterke, DepositPhotos; "Classical decorative elements in baroque style" by Sdart22, DepositPhotos.
Interior Images: "Atlantean Calendar" by Nancy Huett, used with permission; various interior illustrations, schematics, and notes, by Vera Nazarian.

ISBN-13: 978-1-60762-173-7
ISBN-10: 1-60762-173-8

TRADE PAPERBACK EDITION

December 20, 2021

A Publication of
Norilana Books
P. O. Box 209
Highgate Center, VT 05459-0209
www.norilana.com

Printed in the United States of America

The Atlantis Grail
Companion

A Reference Guide to Things and Places for Fans of The Atlantis Grail

The Atlantis Grail Superfan Extras Series

Norilana Books
Science Fiction

www.norilana.com

Other Books by Vera Nazarian

Lords of Rainbow
Dreams of the Compass Rose
Salt of the Air
The Perpetual Calendar of Inspiration
The Clock King and the Queen of the Hourglass
Mayhem at Grant-Williams High (YA)
The Duke in His Castle
After the Sundial
Mansfield Park and Mummies
Northanger Abbey and Angels and Dragons
Pride and Platypus: Mr. Darcy's Dreadful Secret
Vampires are from Venus, Werewolves are from Mars

Cobweb Bride Trilogy:
Cobweb Bride
Cobweb Empire
Cobweb Forest

The Atlantis Grail:
Qualify (Book One)
Compete (Book Two)
Win (Book Three)
Survive (Book Four)

(Forthcoming)

Dawn of the Atlantis Grail (Prequel Series):
Eos (Book One)
Dea (Book Two)
Niktos (Book Three)
Ghost (Book Four)
Starlight (Book Five)

The Atlantis Grail:
The Book of Everything (Book Five)

Dedication

This one's for
Shoelace Girl and *Astra Daimon* Nancy Huett,
with love and gratitude.

The Atlantis Grail
COMPANION

A Reference Guide to Things and Places for Fans of The Atlantis Grail

The Atlantis Grail Superfan Extras Series

VERA NAZARIAN

CONTENTS

Preface

Wixameret, TAG Fan! You hold in your hands the ultimate reference to the universe of *The Atlantis Grail*. . . .

Things, places, rules, customs, stats, definitions, explanations, a complete (to-date) *Atlanteo* language glossary, maps, drawings, schematics, secret nuggets of new information not found anywhere else—it's all here (or mostly, because this universe is huge)! The only thing missing is *dramatis personae*—a comprehensive list of characters—a huge topic which will be covered in a different volume of *The Atlantis Grail Superfan Series*.

And now, prepare to take a deep dive into the universe you love!

ATLANTIS
(ATLANTIDA)
UPPER HEMISPHERE

TheAtlantisGrail.com

CHAPTER 1 – Qualification

The grueling process of Qualification on Earth for those eligible (people between the ages of eleven and twenty) consists of five main stages: **Preliminary Qualification** (also called Pre-Qualification), **Training**, **Semi-Finals**, **Training Continued**, and **Finals**.

Before the process begins, all young people are allowed only two bags (a duffel or small luggage suitcase and a backpack) packed with a basic change of clothing and personal items. If they Qualify, they will not see their families again but be taken directly to board the Atlantean ark-ships and leave Earth forever. If they do not Qualify (or are variously Disqualified and don't die in the process), they return home to face the asteroid disaster and certain death with their families and the rest of humanity.

. . . QUALIFY or DIE! . . .

Preliminary Qualification

On Qualification Day all eligible teens are taken to the local testing facilities called Pre-Qualification Centers, usually designated schools or other public venues, to take a day-long series of unusual tests.

First comes the written knowledge portion. It is followed by a visual preference test of color-based images, the act of drawing a dodecahedron, and a decision-making choice test of preferred "tool"—all designed to place them in their **Color Quadrant**. Next comes a crucial voice test using Atlantean equipment to see if they are able to **carry a tune** (if not, they will never advance to the Training stage, despite passing all other portions of the tests).

Finally, the teens are introduced to **hoverboards** and have to attempt to ride them across a basic distance in the auditorium space. They are also given color tokens where their ID and test data is recorded.

Pre-Candidates who pass all tests have their tokens turn green and are taken to the Regional Qualification Centers or RQCs. They are now officially Candidates for Qualification (among themselves they use the nickname "Candies").

 Want to find out your own Color Quadrant affiliation?
Take the **Color Quadrant Quiz**!
http://www.norilana.com/TAG-Quiz.htm

Training

In just under a year since they first arrived (and mere months after they revealed themselves to Earth authorities), the Atlanteans quickly erected thousands of training compounds all across the country and the world, to serve as Regional Qualification Centers and National Qualification Centers.

Once Candidates arrive at their designated **Regional Qualification Centers** or **RQCs**, they are assigned Dorms based on their Color Quadrant—Red, Blue, Green, or Yellow, then told to follow their Dorm Leaders to their Dorm buildings.

The **Pennsylvania RQC-3** where Gwen Lark and her siblings end up houses 6,023 Candidates. The huge compound has **Twelve Dorms**—three for each Quadrant—administrative office buildings for general Earth staff, and a large Arena Commons superstructure with a running track, pool, cafeteria, other training facilities, rooftop aircraft landing areas, and high-ranking Atlantean offices on upper floors.

Each Dorm building is marked with a solid color square logo of its Quadrant and has five levels—four floors above ground and a basement. First floor ground level contains a Common Area lounge and Cafeteria, second floor is boys' dormitory, third floor is girls' dormitory, fourth floor is Classrooms, and basement level (one floor below ground level) has a Physical Training Area or gym.

Candidates arrive late at night and claim beds on their dormitory floor (first come, first served). Next morning, they attend Orientation presented by their **Dorm Leaders**, and Training officially begins. They are also given the **Rules of Conduct**, curfew times, and told not to engage in sexual behavior with others, on pain of **Disqualification**. In addition, for security reasons, they are now completely cut off from the outside world (and the increasingly dangerous public) and all their digital devices are blocked via firewalls and e-dampers.

Every morning, the Candidates have their **ID tokens** scanned to provide them with a **daily class schedule**, and they are also scanned during each class to mark attendance. When applicable, **demerits** and **credits** are given out by individual **Instructors**, by scanning their ID tokens. The final tallies of all these will count toward their **Standing Scores**.

Training lasts for four weeks, and includes various intensive classes and physical basic training to prepare them for the **Semi-Final Qualification test**.

The classes are taught mostly by Atlantean Instructors, including high ranking **Fleet Pilots**, *astra daimon*, and some Earth staff, and consist of four categories of training:

* Agility Training
* Combat Training
* Atlantis Tech
* Atlantis Culture

Agility includes physical exercise, running, strength training, and hoverboards. **Combat** is Er-Du Martial Arts and specialty weapons training. **Atlantis Tech** is introductory voice training to manipulate orichalcum objects. **Culture** is a class in Atlantean social customs, mores and structure, plus some aspects of history, government, physical sciences, and geography of the colony planet Atlantis itself.

Candidate learning progress and behavior is closely monitored. Instructor recommendations are added to the Standing Scores that everyone is assigned at the end of their training.

Candidate Daily Training Schedule

7:00 AM – wake-up claxon, bathrooms, and breakfast.
8:00 AM – first two classes.
12:00 noon – lunch.
1:00 PM – two more classes.
6:00 PM – dinner.
7:00 PM – rest hour.
8:00 PM – homework or practice.
10:00 PM – lights out, and curfew begins.

At the end of four weeks, the Standing Scores are derived from the following categories, using Gwen's AT scores as an example:

Achievement Total – Score Breakdown – (1-10)

Agility – 3
Voice – 10
Forms – 6
Weapons – 5
Culture – 7

Creativity – 7
Intelligence – 7
Strength – 3
Speed – 4
Flexibility – 4

Balance – 4
Cooperation – 6
Assertion – 5
Endurance – 3
Leadership – 3

Average: 5.13

Finalized Standing Scores determine the order that each Candidate enters the Semi-Finals. After that, having served their purpose, they become meaningless. Gwen's score #4796 determines her place in line for the Semi-Finals, with #1 being best, and #6023 being last place in the RQC.

At the end of training, the Candidates are presented for the first time their **Color Quadrant armbands** to wear on their left upper arm around their sleeve, to show their Quadrant pride.

Semi-Finals

The Semi-Finals are televised world-wide. On the fateful day, Candidates line up according to their Standing score order and enter the Arena Commons where they must race around the track and then choose one of five possible city locations for their grueling ordeal:

> **New York**
> **Chicago**
> **Dallas**
> **Denver**
> **Los Angeles**

Note that these city choices are for the **United States Candidates**, while **other countries** have their own local sites.

Once their choice is made, each Candidate is assigned a **weapon** and, in some cases, a **hoverboard**. Finally, they proceed to the roof of the building where they board Atlantean transport **shuttles** that take them to their chosen locations.

Gwen picks **Los Angeles**.

On board their shuttles, instructions are given.

The Semi-Finals is a **race**, with obstacles customized to take advantage of various local features specific to each city and its surrounding region. In Los Angeles, Candidates are deposited **thirty**

miles from the city center downtown. The task is to **get to the city center** either on foot or by hoverboard, with no other methods permitted, as quickly as possible. They are not allowed to contact with any residents, and may not accept help, including medical or transportation.

During the event there are no Rules of Conduct, and **anything goes**, including violence and murder. Candidates can choose to cooperate with their fellow Candidates and work together in teams, or they can fight each other, using all their skills and training to gain an advantage and get ahead. Meanwhile, everything they do during the Semi-Finals is filmed, and the whole televised event is broadcast locally and worldwide.

The city is divided into **hot zones** and **safe zones**, like concentric **circles**, separated by fence **boundaries** marked by **four-color beacons**, and as Candidates pass each, they are faced with unknown hazards—fire, snipers, killer drones, explosives, booby traps. Their ID tokens act like GPS **trackers** to register their progress in the race. A hot zone is designated by a **red stripe** painted on the interior of the fence boundary.

If at any point a Candidate has had enough—is either too hurt to continue or just decides to give up—they can **Self-Disqualify** by taking off the ID token and pressing the recessed button on the back. It will transmit a signal and mark the Candidate as Disqualified, and send a request for help including an ambulance if needed (and sadly, probably a bus to take them home).

Once Candidates reach the city center downtown, their **final task** is to find a large artificial water reservoir filled with hundreds of **orichalcum batons** (enough for only 20% of the Candidates), and **deliver a baton**—either by means of hoverboard or voice-keying and levitating it while holding on to it—up to any of the low-hovering Atlantean transport **shuttles** that wait for them, and they will have passed Semi-Finals. The shuttles leave at 5:00 PM sharp, so Candidates who miss the shuttles are Disqualified.

The shuttles then take the successful Candidates directly to the National Qualification Center for the next stage of training followed by Finals.

Training Continued

Those who pass the Semi-Finals without being eliminated advance to the **National Qualification Centers (NQCs)** in their respective country and train for another **four weeks** for the **Finals**.

The **United States NQC** is located somewhere in the **Eastern Plains of Colorado**, its exact location undisclosed to the public to keep the Finalists safe from the turbulent world outside. It's an immense compound, the size of a city—a self-sustaining fortress, enclosed from all sides with seventy-five-foot tall, impenetrable steel and concrete walls.

Unlike the RQC, there are only **Four Dorms**, one for each Quadrant (indicated by a solid color square logo). Each one is a huge and long rectangle, similar to an enclosed mall, and stretches for approximately two miles. The buildings are laid out like stripes— between every two Dorms there is another similarly shaped structure designated as a Common Area that is marked with a four-color square logo.

The three Common Area buildings contain a hospital, more cafeterias, training gyms, classrooms, an arena stadium with track and sports training equipment in each, including an immense competition-length swimming pool, administrative offices, and more.

The Dorms resemble airport terminals on the inside and are divided into **Sections**, with each Section housing Candidates from a specific RQC, and their designated **Section Leaders**. There are female and male dormitory areas, Section cafeterias, lounges, small practice pools, and more.

On one side of the complex has a huge **airfield** for Atlantean shuttles.

There are five categories of training for the Finals.

* Agility Training
* Combat Training
* Atlantis Tech
* Atlantis Culture
* Water Survival and Swimming (Water SAS)

Each morning everyone's ID tokens are scanned and their daily class schedule provided. Unlike the Semi-Finals training, all Candidates are also expected to **work in teams**, and there are *individual* and *team* **scores** that will be counted toward their **Finals** score. Each Section is now considered a Team. For example, Gwen is in Section Fourteen, so she is on the Yellow Quadrant Team Fourteen.

Candidates are assigned *one hundred starting points* at the beginning of training. In order to pass the Finals, Candidates will need to have **more than** one hundred points at the *end* of the Finals Day.

Instructors can issue demerits or credits throughout the four weeks of training which the Candidates can see when their ID tokens are scanned. They take the sum total of points on the last day of training into the Finals and these accumulated points become the individual's personal property.

They can **keep them** all or **share them** with others. A portion of each Candidate's points, or the entirety, can be transferred to the team as a whole or to other individual team members. A poor *team score* will reduce the final points total for all the Candidates on that team, regardless of individual high scores.

Finals

Finals Day takes place on the last day of the four intensive weeks of training. Candidates are given instructions the day before, by their Section Leaders.

Candidates must arrive in the Section lobby by 6:30 AM. Their ID tokens are scanned, final points tallied and announced, and they receive their final Team assignments. For example, Gwen has 185 Final Points and is on Team USA Fourteen-C. They have less than fifteen minutes to eat, then at 6:45 AM they exit their dorms and go directly to the airfield.

No later than 7:00 AM, Candidates must board the Atlantean shuttles assigned to their team.

Once the shuttles are in flight, final instructions are given by the Atlantean shuttle pilots including the following explanation.

Thousands of years ago during the time of the original Atlantis on Earth, ancient Atlanteans built a **major transportation network** between the continent of Atlantis and the other continents bordering the Atlantic Ocean—a complex system of subterranean caves and tunnels, allowing secret travel underneath the ocean from Atlantis to other lands.

The tunnels connect a series of sunken chambers that get flooded and drained by means of locks and floodgates. In order to avoid cave-ins, only a few chambers are filled with air at a time. The mass of water in all the rest keeps the tunnels and caverns intact under the immense weight of the earth and the ocean.

The entry points to these tunnels are located at numerous places all around the shores of the Atlantic. And they all connect in the center, right underneath Ancient Atlantis itself—the modern-day area spanning Bermuda and the Bahamas.

On Finals Day, Candidates all around the world are taken to **various entry points** along the shores of the **Atlantic**.

Gwen is taken somewhere off-shore between **Jacksonville, Florida** and the former location of the long-flooded **Florida Keys**.

The exact starting times at all points around the Atlantic are synchronized, so that every entry-point site gets **34 hours** to complete the task.

Shuttles dive underneath the ocean and emerge in **subterranean caverns** drained of water and filled with air, initiating the **ancient transport system** of **locks and floodgates**.

Once inside the first cavern, each Candidate in the shuttle is faced with the point of no return. As soon as they step outside, they commit to participating in the Finals competition and **forfeit their lives** and their choice in the matter. Unlike the Semi-Finals, there are no means of rescuing people from the middle of the tunnel system once its sequence is activated.

This is the last chance to Self-Disqualify. Candidates can remove their ID tokens, press the recessed button on the back, remain in their seats and wait. They will be returned back to the National Qualification Center and discharged to go home.

Candidates who bravely choose to proceed with the Finals are provided with a **hoverboard**, a single **weapon** of their Quadrant, a **flashlight**, two **flares**, and a small **pack** containing **food and water** for one day.

They also receive full control of their final points, to be used at their discretion. The owner initiates the transfer—pressing their ID token and that of the other person, and announcing the number of points to be granted. Candidates cannot take points from others, only receive them.

From that moment on, Candidates act both as an individual and as a team.

All **Sections** are divided into **four Teams, A, B, C,** and **D,** in order of achievement, as measured by points. This determines their time of entry into the cavern system—first, second, third, or last. Team A has a 1.5-hour advantage, Team B has a one-hour advantage, and Team C has a half-hour advantage over Team D. Every Team must wait for its turn.

Candidates have approximately **33.3 hours** to cross the distance of **1,000 miles** underneath the ocean floor, on **hoverboards**. The task is achievable if they maintain a minimum rate of **30 miles an hour**.

Every **half hour**, the locks and **floodgates** activate, starting a new **"lockout wave"**—water begins flooding the chamber the Candidates are in from the next chamber in the sequence. At that time the gates between the two adjacent chambers are open, allowing passage from one to the other, while the water drains. Candidates must pace themselves to always stay ahead of the floodgates, else the gates close with them inside, the chamber floods, and they drown.

The floodgates are marked with **four-color beacons**, and Candidate ID tokens are scanned as they pass. All team members must work together since the number of **surviving members** positively contributes to the individual's **cumulative score**—an incentive to help keep their teammates alive.

Once Candidates reach the final cavern chamber—the immense **central hub** underneath **Ancient Atlantis**, somewhere around present-day Bermuda—they must to rise to the surface through a wide tunnel carved out of an underwater mountain. Every Candidate team from everywhere around the world converges into the same single cavern for the final sprint race for the Qualification spots.

The original tunnel opening, many feet underwater, has been retrofitted to extend to the surface of the Atlantic Ocean. Only *half* of the remaining Candidates can **Qualify**.

Candidates who reach the shuttles on time need to have a minimum of **100 individual points** plus a **minimum team average number** for their entire team. The number of missing or dead members is subtracted from the team average number.

As soon as the last shuttle is filled to capacity, the doors close. Anyone not onboard does not Qualify.

The next day, at 8:00 PM exactly, the shuttles depart Earth.

Fun Fact: The explosion that rocks the central hub cavern—attributed for most of the story to Earth terrorist group Terra Patria (and possibly the Sunset Alliance, or other chaotic rebel group)—is in fact caused by the Atlanteans themselves who use the opportunity of general mayhem to make another attempt at closing the ancient *quantum dimensional rift* that is located near that spot.

CHAPTER 2 – Atlantean Society

All aspects of society on Imperial *Atlantida*, the oldest nation on the colony planet, are deeply rooted in **class hierarchy**.

Below *nobility* (designated by numbered generations of noble rank), the general population consists of *commoners*—referred to either as **Civilians** (non-military), or military **Fleet personnel**—and elevated **Citizens** who have earned the **right to vote** and hold higher social positions of **power** and distinction. All Nobility are Citizens, but not all Citizens are Nobles.

Over time, the **three major divisions** of society into *nobility*, *citizens*, and *commoners*, have produced insurmountable differences in lifestyle aspirations, achievements, and possible choices for individuals.

In order to break out of their static social castes, and achieve their life goals, some commoners take an extreme risk and put their lives on the line by entering the **Games of the Atlantis Grail** as a Contender. Surviving the Four Stages of competition and becoming a Champion in one of the Ten Categories is the only sure way of attaining **Citizenship**.

Nobility and Rules of Title Inheritance

- All original members of Ancient Atlantean nobility that fled from Earth are Citizens.

- All newly designated members of nobility are Citizens.

- Children of nobility inherit titles from their noble parents.

- When both parents are Citizens but not nobility, children inherit the Citizenship from their parents.

- When one parent is a Citizen and the other a commoner, their children do not inherit Citizenship.

- When a Citizen or commoner marries a noble, they gain the equivalent rank of nobility by marriage, unless they remarry (this does not affect the rank standing of their children through the original marriage).

- Members of all the Priesthoods come from all walks of life and their official standing is unaffected by their sacred rank. While some might advance by other means, even the First Priests with significant influence may remain commoners without the right to vote.

- Nobility rank begins with "first generation."

- Nobility may be granted to deserving individuals by the Imperator for extraordinary service to the country or other accomplishments and distinctions. This is done very infrequently.

- If a commoner marries into the Imperial Kassiopei Family, they automatically become a Citizen and the Imperial Consort (which comes with automatic nobility), and all members of their immediate family (parents and siblings) become Citizens. The immediate family is also granted the first rank of nobility.

The Four Cornerstones of Atlantis

The **four divisions of labor** on the ancient ark-ships fleeing Earth 12,500 years ago evolve over the centuries into four unique *social allegiances* of personal dignity and pride.

They have now become the **cornerstones** of all aspects of Atlantean culture, personal dignity, and achievement. Each one is associated with a **Color**, and in social situations is referred to as a **Quadrant**.

Red Cornerstone (Quadrant)

Passion – Aggression – Anger – Force
Musical Key – Major
Pilot Role – Drive/Propulsion
Symbol – Sword
Weapons – Blade, Edge

Blue Cornerstone (Quadrant)

Leadership – Control – Reason – Analysis
Musical Key – Minor
Pilot Role – Organizational Balance, Command Center
Symbol – Pen
Weapons – Firearms

Green Cornerstone (Quadrant)

Endurance – Patience – Resistance – Strength
Musical Key – Flat
Pilot Role – Brake
Symbol – Shield
Weapons – Armor

Yellow Cornerstone (Quadrant)

Creativity – Originality – Curiosity – Inspiration
Musical Key – Sharp
Pilot Role – Navigation/Guidance
Symbol – Map
Weapons – Nets and Cords

First Year Cadets in Fleet School, and civilian children in other schools, are known as *kefarai*. All are required to choose their Quadrant affiliation by the end of their First Year which culminates in the **Quadrant Choosing Ceremony**.

On that memorable evening, before the **First-Year pins** are handed out, the whole *kefarai* class gathers in the school courtyard or assembly hall. All students are given **blank orbs** to hold, which then are lit on cue with their **chosen color** of internal flame.

As soon as the individual flames are lit, students are permitted to put on their new **color armbands**. The Quadrant affiliation armband goes on the **left upper arm**, and the folds keeping the fabric in place are clever and simple.

Everyone's Quadrant choices are usually anticipated in advance, reflecting their personality, spirit, and tendencies.

 Want to find out your own Color Quadrant affiliation?
Take the **Color Quadrant Quiz!**
http://www.norilana.com/TAG-Quiz.htm

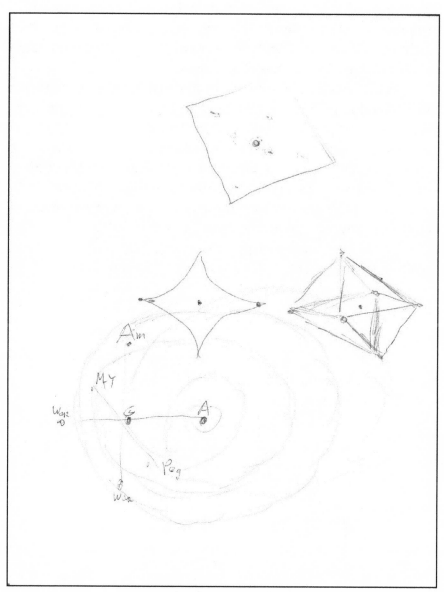

Astroctadra Ghost Moon Alignment

Astroctadra

The ***astroctadra*** is an ancient **four-point star** symbol that is a common traditional design element permeating all aspects of Atlantean culture. The Cadet pins worn by the Qualified Earth teens are their first example of this classic shape.

The *astroctadra* can be a flat **two-dimensional shape** or a **three-dimensional object**. It is reminiscent of the Great Square, the cube geometric shape, and even the Four Quadrants.

When modeled in 3D, it's fundamentally a distorted cube—a type of polygon that is an **octahedron**, a 3D shape with **six vertices** and **eight sides**. This shape is also known as a *square bipyramid.*

From another perspective, the *astroctadra* shape is a molecule of **sulfur hexafluoride** (greenhouse gas, electrical insulator).

Various *astroctadra*-shaped alignments and physical objects such as windows and keys play a vital role in the series.

Find the moon around a star,
Ride the Pegasus too far.

Find the star around a moon,
Meet your love by afternoon.

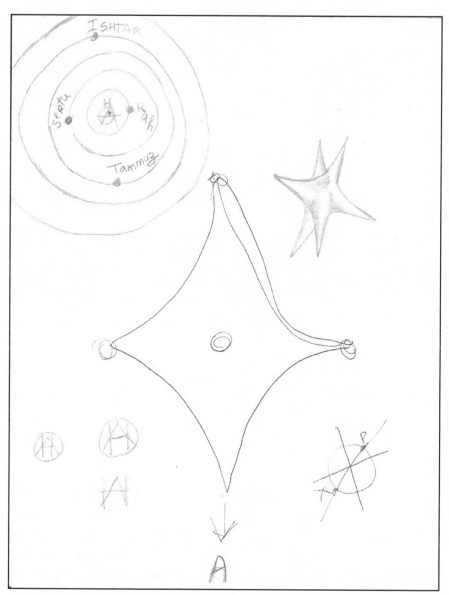

Astroctadra Helios System Planetary Alignment

The Atlantis Grail and the Ra Disk

The Atlantis Grail is a mysterious monumental object on display in Poseidon, the capital city of Imperial *Atlantida*, in the arena of the Atlantis Grail Stadium downtown. It is shaped like an immense shallow goblet, stands more than **two hundred meters** tall, and marks the first **Landing Site** of the oldest colony on the surface of the planet Atlantis.

The popular notion is that the **Atlantis Grail** is a national symbol of everything the Atlantean society stands for—both ancient tradition and new modern innovation. It embodies the spirit of the New World which the Atlanteans now inhabit. Initially, not much is known about its origins, only that it has a "sibling" monument in the form of the **Ra Disk** located on the opposite side of the globe in the capital city of New Deshret. The ancient symbol of New Deshret, the Ra Disk is a huge golden disk carved from the slope of Dubutaat Mountain and plated in gold, as big as the Atlantis Grail.

"The Ra Disk, stupid Earth girl. It's New Deshret's equivalent of our Atlantis Grail. It's a big-ass monument in their capital city."

—Anu Vei

During various ceremonies held in the Stadium, the Grail "sings"—usually at the command of the **Imperator** who voice-keys it and issues ceremonial sequences to it. The monument **resonates** with a powerful sound that is heard for miles in the surrounding neighborhoods. In reality this ceremonial showmanship is a disguise for the annual maintenance of the **Great Quantum Shield**, an ancient duty of the Kassiopei rulers who do this to protect the planet from the threat of the ancient alien enemy, *"They."*

Eventually it is revealed that the Atlantis Grail monument is not a monument at all, but the **uppermost section** of a very ancient, very deeply **buried ark-ship** (the Vimana) that brought the original Atlanteans to the colony planet and landed in the middle of what is now downtown Poseidon. The bulk of the ship extends far underneath the *Stadion* which marks the Landing Site of the first Colony.

The Ra Disk is not a carving but a **portion** of that same ship. It fits precisely over the top of the Grail to create a **great golden sphere**—a **resonance chamber**.

More is revealed once the Ghost Moon is added in the mix—they are all one set of quantum-entangled structures.

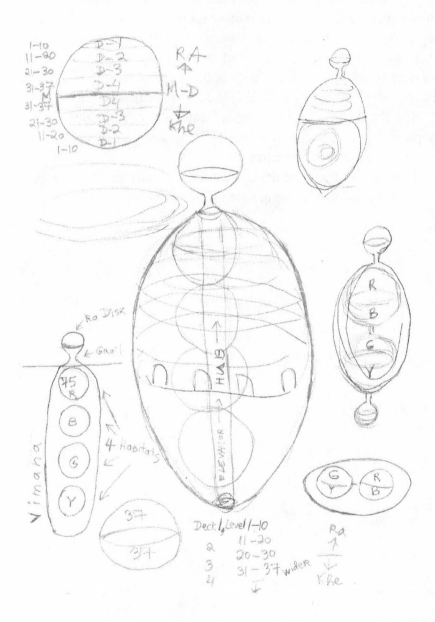

Ancient Ark-Ship Vimana

Governments of Atlantis

There are fewer than **seventy nations** currently recognized on the colony planet Atlantis. Many of them are pure **democracies**, others hereditary **democratic monarchies**, and others are **republics**. In nearly every instance, the governments of these nations are comprised of elected representatives, and their hereditary rulers (imperial or otherwise) are mostly figureheads, and have no control over the workings of the government or its laws.

It is understood that there are no tyrants, no despots on modern day Atlantis. Such a thing is considered an ancient barbaric anachronism. Atlanteans in every nation define and choose their own governing body, and their laws are fair and just, for all citizens. In reality, this varies in nuance and degree.

Imperial Atlantida Government

The oldest nation, Imperial *Atlantida*, is officially an **Imperial Democracy**. By modern law and public understanding, the Imperator and the **Imperial Family**—members of the powerful ancient **Kassiopei Dynasty**—are technically considered to be mostly inspirational and ceremonial figureheads. Their main duty is to officially preside over public spectacles and traditional events. Meanwhile, councils of elected officials run the government.

The Poseidon **Imperial Executive Council**, or **IEC**, is the official ruling governing body of *Atlantida*, together with the **Archaeon Imperator** who is technically a **figurehead** with the limited power of a ***single vote*** on the Council. However, because the Imperial Family owns much of the nation's land, the Imperator's real influence is far greater. Furthermore, the Imperator can choose to be very active, try to influence other members of the IEC, attend all the IEC meetings, and use every opportunity to exercise a large measure of governing power.

It is therefore vital that the IEC always remain the legally dominant branch of government, serving to offset and balance the insidious power of the Imperator.

The Imperial Executive Council

Throughout history, the IEC has recognized the **Ennead**, a special group of *nine core members*, holding double or **weighted votes**. However, currently there is no active Ennead on the IEC, so all members' votes are considered equal.

The number of members also varies throughout history. The current number is *twelve*, plus the Imperator who casts the thirteenth deciding vote in case of a tie. Whenever the number of members is an *odd number* (so that the addition of the Imperial vote makes it an even number), and the vote is split down the middle, the Imperator is permitted by law to cast a *double vote* so that he can resolve the tie.

The IEC members have distinctive formal attire for Court occasions and Council meetings. Both men and women wear *long gold and white robes* and *gold filigree skull caps*.

The following are active IEC members at the time of the Earth refugee arrival:

- Imperator Romhutat Kassiopei
- Imperial Fleet Commander Manakteon Resoi
- Imperial Crown Prince Aeson Kassiopei
- Lord Arao Hetepheret
- Dame Tammuz Akten
- Lady Ishtar Sitamun
- Lord Asiwet
- Council Member Amasis
- Council Member Gobu
- Lady Iela Nastasen
- Council Member Takhat
- First Priest Shirahtet
- Atlantis Central Agency (ACA) Director Hijep Tiofon

In addition, the following *non-members* are often called upon for advisory recommendations, but have no voting power:

- Science and Technology Agency (STA) Director Rovat Bennu
- Legal and Correctional Agency (LCA) Arch Corrector Peleset Frawei
- Consul Suval Denu

IEC Member Political Positions

At the time of the pending alien threat, this is the described political climate among the different members in the IEC, with strong and contrary positions held by specific individuals:

- Mobilize the Fleet **(Everyone)**.

- Keep it all secret from the public **(Imperator, Council Member Takhat, First Priest Shirahtet, ACA Director Hijep Tiofon)**.

- Quickly select and train in an accelerated manner the best Earth Cadets for Star Pilot Corps duty **(Lord Arao Hetepheret and Dame Tammuz Akten)**.

- Tell the general public of Atlantis about the alien threat **(Lord Asiwet)**.

- Tell only the Earth refugees about the alien threat and keep it secret from the public **(Lady Ishtar Sitamun)**.

- Deploy Atlantean-only forces, was anti-Earth mission **(Council Member Amasis)**.

- Increase and improve monitoring surveillance for aliens; listen for them via sensitive **sound** equipment, look for them in the skies, underneath the oceans **(Council Member Gobu)**.

- Comply with the aliens demands **(Lord Arao Hetepheret and Dame Tammuz Akten)**.

- Prepare for possible evacuation from Atlantis, escape again to the stars, so search for suitable new planet far away **(Lady Iela Nastasen)**.

- Return to Earth to pick up more people and resources before the asteroid hits. Earth UN might be an ally. **(ACA Director Hijep Tiofon)**.

- Pool the resources of Earth and Atlantis against the common enemy **(Aeson)**.

Other Nations Governments

While Imperial *Atlantida* is strongly rooted in class hierarchy, its closest neighbors are more democratic. **Eos-Heket** is presided by the **Oratorat** who is an elected official similar to a president or prime minister. **Ubasti** has a ruling council of nine elected representatives called the **Ennead**, all having equal voices and votes, and whose **First Speaker** has no more power but merely speaks on behalf of the Ennead.

At the same time, on the opposite hemisphere, the other superpower, **New Deshret**, is very similar to Imperial *Atlantida*, and is also an Imperial Democracy. The **Pharikon** of New Deshret is the analogue of the **Imperator**, except the ruling family Dynasty there is **Heru**, and they are slightly more restrictive, with their council having only half the governing power of the Pharikon.

Other lesser nations such as Ptahleon, Shuria, Bastet, Ankh-Tawi, and Weret have hereditary rulers called **Rai**, the equivalent of "king." Each Rai is usually supported in governing by a council, and there are no absolute power holders.

Similarly, even smaller hereditary rulers are called **Hetmet**, such as the ones in Khenneb and Qurartu.

There is also the **Crown Hereret** in Vai Naat, a hereditary royal similar to a duke, and granted primary "Crown" powers by a family vote from a pool of other regional Hererets.

Top Twelve Atlantean Nations and their Rulers

Imperial Atlantida – Archaeon Imperator Romhutat Kassiopei
New Deshret – Pharikon Areviktet Heru
Ubasti – First Speaker of the Ennead of Ubasti, Anen Qur
Eos-Heket – Oratorat Kephasa Sewu
Vai Naat – Crown Hereret Wilem Paeh
Ptahleon – Rai Inevar Arelik
Shuria – Rai Osuo Menebuut
Bastet – Rai Duu Valam
Qurartu – Hetmet Qedeh Adamer
Ankh-Tawi – Rai Mialoor Isaret
Weret – Rai Shebion Neph
Khenneb – Hetmet Bakar Ramajet

Law Enforcement

Atlantean justice is methodical and thorough. The first example of it is shown in **Qualify** when the Correctors arrive on the scene after the tragic shuttle explosion incident to start the criminal investigation. They intimidate and question everyone.

And as Gwen discovers when she is wrongfully arrested as a suspect, she *loses all rights* including the right to a lawyer. The only thing she can do is to offer proof of her innocence.

Correctors are both detectives and police officers combined. On Atlantis, they are under the jurisdiction of the **Legal and Correctional Agency (LCA)** which is comparable to an Earth Police Department. The current equivalent of Police Chief is **Arch Corrector** Peleset Frawei, who is assigned to oversee all law enforcement in Poseidon.

In the greater Poseidon area including the Golden Bay coast, the land-and-sea law enforcement is performed by **Coastal Correctors**, with a **Coastal Nomarch** in charge. They also report to the LCA.

The **Poseidon Central Correctional Facility** is the largest prison in the area. The **Warden** is in charge of several Correctors, and Logan Sangre works for him.

Atlantean laws are strict and ancient. The ultimate punishment is execution, or life in prison under terrible conditions—sometimes given to prisoners as an ironic choice. There are other lesser punishments that run the gamut of various years in prison or brief community service. However, there are sufficient loopholes and complexity that skillful **Arbiters** are required to handle each case. Arbiters are the equivalent of Earth attorneys or lawyers.

Cases are heard at the **Imperial Court of Law** building (with architectural elements of a grand ziggurat and a stepped pyramid) located in the business district, downtown Poseidon.

Basic Social Norms and Everyday Life

The following are some basic aspects of everyday Atlantean life—the kinds of entertainment they have, their equivalent of films and television, books, games, and activities.

Atlanteans love to *tell stories through music*, so their equivalent of **opera** is a very big deal in Poseidon. So is their equivalent of *soap opera*. They watch a variety of shows on the various network video feeds, attend concerts and theatrical performances, museums, and other public entertainment.

Various media networks proliferate—some strongly government-controlled, such as the **Helios-Ra Imperial Poseidon Network (HRIPN)** also known as **Hel-Ra Network**.

Atlanteans also love *sports* such as **skyball** (a team ball game where players on and off hoverboards must keep a ball up in the air) and *betting* on the outcomes. See *CHAPTER 12 – The Games of the Atlantis Grail* for the exploration of their favorite Green Season obsession—watching the Games non-stop and gambling on every aspect of them.

Of course, the serious stuff is also interesting. One of the aspects of Atlantean society is the early age at which children begin to study and assume adult responsibilities. The deep underlying reasons for this are explained in **Survive**.

On their journey to Atlantis, Instructor Nilara Gradat explains to the Earth students during their Culture classes:

> *"You will find that we have very young people doing work that you might find surprising. If you think this Fleet is full of teens, wait till you see our towns and cities and the kinds of business trades that are handled by your peers."*

Money and Currency

The official national currency of Imperial *Atlantida* is the **iret** (singular) or **iretar** (plural), which is available as metal coins, roll-up scroll bills, and digital versions. The conversion rate with Earth currency has not been determined, and it is not really comparable to the British pound sterling, Australian dollar, Canadian dollar, or the Euro. In general, it converts much higher in value than a US dollar.

There is a banking system with private and national banks with branches in different areas, and people have personal accounts.

During the Games of the Atlantis Grail, the Champions are awarded huge monetary prizes from a common deposit account called the **Common Earnings Grail** which consists of a share of the revenue from that season's betting by the public and other Games related income.

Every year it holds a very generous sum. The divided winnings are deposited in the Champions' personal credit accounts on the night of the Final Ceremony, and usually consist of over ten million *iretar* for each of the Top Ten. Champions may spend every single *iret* in any manner they desire, at any institution or venue.

Gwen soon finds out she is not just an independently wealthy woman, but she's filthy rich.

I enter a secret passcode in addition to a biometric scan to access my Common Earnings Grail personal credit account, and sure enough, the sum deposited there in my own name is **10,370,407 iretar**. I'm not clear on what the conversion rate would be to Earth United States dollars or Euros or Yuan, but I know that it's a huge sum, maybe even comparable to a billion dollars.

When Kokayi Jeet has his parade in the streets of Themisera, everyone gets to throw *iretar* coins to the people along the parade route.

To provide the baskets of coins for the parade, the local financial institutions have to come up with so many physical coins that, according to Kokayi, he "probably cleaned out at least twenty currency branches in the area."

Thousands of *iretar* are tossed to the people by Kokayi and the other Champions riding in his Parade.

Unfortunately, *Mamai* Jeet, his mother, is not too impressed by her son's "wasteful" habits.

Good thing Kokayi has so much *iretar* that it doesn't matter.

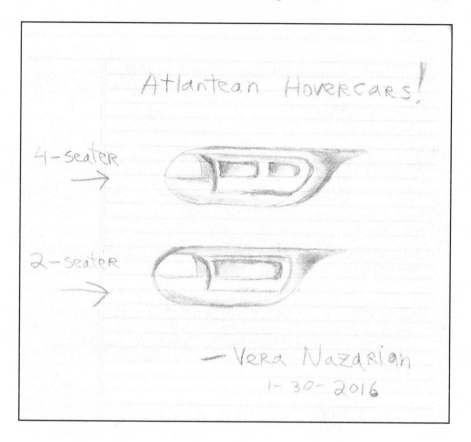

Opportunities for the Earthies

By the time the Earth refugees arrive on Atlantis, they've had a year to prepare for possible careers on their new home planet. Toward the end of their journey, they have received career counseling and global placement.

Instructors give an inspirational rundown of career options for technically inclined Civilians.

The Earthies are told that they can apply for entry level jobs in most of Atlantean industries, as soon they land. Or they can enroll in more advanced courses to get better positions. The recommendation is to take that entry level work and at the same time attend extra training courses in their off hours, especially if they decide to stay and make their home in the capital, Poseidon, or the provinces.

In short, they have many options, and as Earth refugees who have proven their various talents and skills simply by Qualifying for Atlantis, they will be in demand.

Upon arrival, many of them indeed find interesting and diverse opportunities.

Some of the Earthies get jobs at Heri Agriculture (a major agri-corporation), at the Poseidon HQ, working with the Earth Seed Bank, in the bio-analysis division. Atlantean staple food crops are based on ancient Earth wheat and barley, so they get to do DNA analysis and compare the Atlantean varieties that evolved under alien conditions and the modern Earth native specimens they just brought from Earth.

Other opportunities at Heri include cultivation and crop production design tech, such as the design of crop planting patterns (horizontal and vertical), exploring the use of physical 3D space. Atlanteans plant not only in the soil but in the air (aeroponically) and in the water (hydroponically) as they did on the ark-ships.

Others Earthies obtain work in manufacturing defense textiles, a military industry requiring higher clearance (the Atlantean equivalent of a government military defense contractor). It includes the manufacturing of fabrics and weapons based on textiles.

There are also teaching positions at the Fleet Cadet School for special skills such as LM Forms, or work at the Poseidon Correctional facilities.

Meanwhile, for some there are positions in the newly opened Earth antiquities wing of the Imperial Poseidon Museum. Earth historians and specialists are a welcome addition—to research and lecture and even teach classes to the public, and occasionally observe a ridiculous level of competition and hostility among other museums.

"Have you tried asking those pedantic *chazufs* at the Imperial Poseidon Museum? I assure you, it is highly likely they can assist you with your *hoohvak* request because, once and for all, we at Sekar Mehet do *not* have any *shar-ta-haak* Mask of your *shebet* Tutankhamen!"

Many refugees find jobs with small businesses, pursuing crafts that interest them, or work in other fields such as medical, transportation, fashion, engineering, retail, the food industry, and more. The more enterprising begin positioning themselves to own their own businesses and become entrepreneurs.

Races and Ethnicities

Atlanteans are as culturally and ethnically diverse as the population of ancient Earth was 12,500 years ago, and the colonists and their descendants are made up of a mixture of all races.

The ruling elite classes tend to be darker skinned, such as the golden bronze-skinned Kassiopei Family (comparable to the royalty of Ancient Egypt). The Heru Family possess the river-red-clay skin coloration and features found in people from Mesoamerica. Many of the High Court nobility would currently be identified as people of color (brown or black), such as the Ruo Family, and just as many other noble families of long generations carry genes for the epicanthic eye folds and Earth Asian physical traits possessed by Quoni Enutat and Tiliar Vahad.

Meanwhile, the very poor commoners from remote locations outside urban centers tend to be lighter skinned, like Anu Vei's impoverished fish village family.

Atlanteans are imperfect human beings after all, and there are plenty of problematic things about their societies in the various nations around the globe. However, racial or ethnic tensions have not developed to a significant degree. Instead, over the centuries, the real tensions are class and hierarchy-based.

Love and Marriage Customs

Romantic love on Atlantis includes unions between *individuals of any sex or gender*. In fact, there is no discrimination or prejudice against same-sex unions or non-binary individuals (and persons who are intersex from birth are considered especially fortunate and blessed by the gods, and in some places are revered for their wisdom—very much as it was on Earth in ancient times). It is an absolute non-issue in the general population. The only exception is when it comes to major noble estates and *rank inheritance*, in which case *procreation* comes into play and can unfortunately prevent true love unions.

Unlike on Earth, there are different sorts of legal unions. Some are like a traditional marriage, others are primarily for companionship and affection, while imperial or royal families may create unions for procreation, lineage and family continuation purposes, to perpetuate dynastic connections.

Normal everyday Atlanteans may love anyone they choose, and legally mate and bond for love and attraction. Those who are wealthier and more powerful may be "gently" pressured into marriages for purposes of combining families—to enlarge property, or expand businesses. Members of the highest nobility are the least fortunate, being rigidly constrained by the demands of their family continuation.

"I don't want to talk about the troll anymore."

—Laronda Aimes

Generally, the courtship and dating process begins around the age of **twelve** Atlantean years, which is the equivalent of **sixteen** Earth years. However, Atlantean social norms do not encourage intimate relations before true physical and emotional maturity.

The legal age of adulthood on Atlantis is **sixteen** years, the equivalent of **twenty and a half** Earth Years.

Relationship taboos include lack of consent, child marriage, and incest, all of which are illegal.

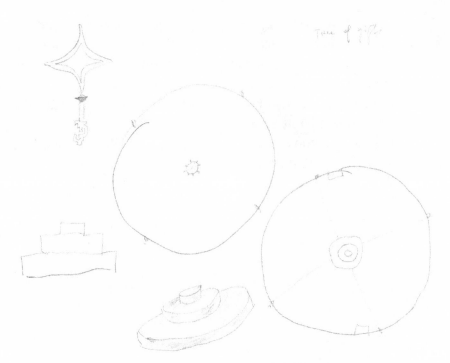

The Tree of Gifts, Key to the Room of Childhood Secrets.

Traditional Wedding

Once a couple makes a formal commitment to each other, a wedding date is set. (There are some exceptions especially in polyamorous relationships involving more than two individuals, but usually these are not traditionally formalized.)

In case of upper-class weddings, if inheritance or property is involved, the families settle pre-nuptial agreements before the couple can "choose" each other.

The **wedding ceremony** is performed by a **Priest and Priestess of Amrevet-Ra** (hired by means of a generous donation to their priesthood, shrine, or temple). Afterwards, there is feast of families and their guests. That night the *Amrevet* **Night** ceremony takes place where the couple consummates their physical intimacy for the first time as spouses. The next day—or a period up to three days—is a holiday for the couple, but after that brief time off they return to work or their ordinary lives. The honeymoon, or *Amrevet* **Days**, is not taken until approximately eight months later.

Virginity is not a requirement except for the highest-ranking nobility and royalty, where again it's merely a matter of strict genetic breeding selection and carefully planned traditional procreation.

It must be added that Atlantean medical technology and society allows genetic manipulation. Only genetic material is needed for fully viable embryos to be made in a lab for any couple in the general population. But again, the highest ranks of nobility and royalty insist on the traditional methods of bringing forth children.

The most formal traditional weddings require many ceremonies and intense planning. The **Bridal Events** and **Bridegroom Events** begin two months before the wedding.

For example, Gwen Lark undergoes a series of veritable "ordeals" when working with the Venerable Therutat Nuudri, the First Priestess of Amrevet-Ra who oversees all high ceremonial matters regarding Imperial nuptials.

The **Imperial Bridal Book** (an antique, bejeweled scroll) presented to the Bride contains a bullet-point list of **required activities**. And the Bride must carefully follow this schedule. There is a similar rulebook for the Bridegroom that has to be read and memorized by the time of the Wedding.

Some of Gwen's required Bridal activities are:

- Ladies of the Court reception
- Choose Flowers
- Choose Song
- Bride Show Day
- Gifts Assembly
- Media Interviews
- Meet with the Imperatris
- Memorize the Imperial Consort Protocol.
- Be Fitted for the Wedding Dress and *Amrevet* Dress.

What is an *Amrevet* Dress, you might ask? Here is how Aeson explains it in **Survive**:

> *Aeson's gaze rests on me and intensifies. His own face flushes, as he says softly, "The* Amrevet *Dress is worn later—at night. And it's not exactly a dress."*

The three days leading up to the Wedding are particularly important, and are reserved by tradition:

- **Final Dress Fitting** scheduled three days before the Wedding to ensure time for alterations.
- **Family *dea* meal** occurs two days before the Wedding and marks the Joining of the two Families.
- **Fasting and Cleansing Day** takes place the day before the Wedding.

In addition, the Bride and Groom must abstain from physical contact with each other, to minimize temptation and remain chaste until the Wedding.

"Our first day, and I am already undone by you."

—Aeson Kassiopei

After a Day of Fasting, on the morning of the Wedding Day, the Bride and Bridegroom are escorted separately by priestesses and priests to the venue in a procession.

The **Wedding Ceremony** includes:

- Invocation by the Priests of Amrevet-Ra.
- Naming of the Bride and Bridegroom.
- Surrender of the couple by their Families to themselves and each other.
- Joining of Palms to ignite the Fire of Amrevet-Ra.
- Songs of the Bride and Bridegroom to channel the Fire.
- Speaking of the Will for the Union (the pledge).
- Lighting of the Sacred Flames around the altar chalice in a circle.
- Singing *Eoseiara* in unison.
- Proclamation of the Union by the Priests of Amrevet-Ra.
- Giving of the Light by the Families and Friends in affirmation.
- Final Blessing of the Priests of Amrevet-Ra.

Fortunately, Gwen is permitted to incorporate some Earth traditions into her very intricate and formal Atlantean wedding ceremony, such as the exchange of wedding rings (Aeson's surprise for her), the kiss, and the wearing of "something old, something new, something borrowed, something blue."

And then, of course, there is Gwen's unique four-layer Wedding Dress!

Afterwards, the Newlywed Couple ride together in a procession to the Reception and Feast venue. Everything around them is decorated with the Bride's chosen Flowers.

"So. . . . Which one of you will dance with me?"

—Xelio Vekahat

At the Reception there is food, dancing—including the traditional *irephuru* circle dance—and strong *shedehur* to drink. Finally, the Couple leaves the Reception to begin their *Amrevet* Night.

Amrevet Days – The Atlantean Honeymoon

On Atlantis, *amrevet* days are the Atlantean equivalent of a honeymoon, except taken half a year later. Some of the fun aspects of this custom are the *escape* and the *secret locations*.

At the end of the first eight months after the Wedding, the newlyweds "flee" their normal life and "hide" together in a delightful secret place of their own choosing, for continued intimacy, at the same time letting their families and friends know only the general whereabouts.

Contemporary Atlanteans don't have the same concept of "honeymoon" that many contemporary Earth cultures do. Instead of going on a multi-day or even multi-week trip to some romantic destination for sightseeing, lovemaking, and special time together, Atlanteans take up to three days after the Wedding to relax and be intimate in the comfort of their own homes, and then settle back into their normal daily lives. The time immediately after the Wedding emphasizes the concept of hearth and *home*.

However, there's another tradition called "*amrevet* days," which takes place at the end of the **first eight months** of their married life. It involves a sneaky escape from friends and family to a secret destination for some much-needed privacy for the couple. There is a long-distance trip involved, to reinforce their commitment to one another—a kind of renewal of vows. Many couples choose this time to conceive children.

The Imperial tradition is only slightly different. In addition to the Imperial Crown Prince and His Wife enjoying a private "day off" after their Wedding Day to establish their new intimate *home* in each other's hearts and each other's company, the entire nation gets a holiday.

Zero Gravity Dances

Can you imagine dancing in low gravity and then zero gravity? What an indescribable feeling it must be, flying to music!

Zero-G dancing is one of the most **ancient cultural traditions** on Atlantis, and it stems from the original colonization period. When the Ancient Atlantean refugees from Earth arrived on this new planet, they had few means of entertainment, and Zero-G dancing happened to be something they did on their ships along their way. When they landed and established that first colony, the tradition remained. Since then, all Atlantean dance halls and entertainment centers have **gravity manipulation**—one of the few traditions that were never outlived.

Fun Fact: In ancient times the Zero-G Dances were *never* held inside ship Resonance Chambers. The reason is revealed in the prequel series.

And now, in 2047 (Year 9770 on Atlantis), this tradition is recreated for the modern Earth refugees. There are **four Zero-G Dances** held on the ark-ships during Gwen's journey, one dance held for each Atlantean season which the corresponding Quadrant hosts.

For example, since the first season on board the ark-ships is Blue, the Blue Quadrant hosts the first Zero-G Dance.

The dance itself happens inside the great spherical chamber in the heart of each ship—the **Resonance Chamber**. Each Quadrant decorates the interior based on the theme of the Dance, but everything must be in shades of that specific **Quadrant Color**, including everyone's attire (the only exception being the Fleet white dress uniform).

Fun Fact: During the very first Zero-G Dance, some of the Earth teens broke tradition and wore black formal wear, but they were gently reprimanded afterwards, and from that point on stuck to the appropriate Quadrant Color.

So where does this fancy attire come from? People design their own, and the ark-ship 3D printers manufacture the outfits to order!

People get dressed up in gorgeous formal wear of their choice and invite dates—friends, family, significant others. Traditionally, individuals get to invite anyone they like when it's *their* Quadrant's turn to host the dance. Otherwise, it is most appropriate to wait to be invited.

And now, a little about the venue. . . .

The Resonance Chamber is primarily used to drive the ship. However, the Resonance Chamber also happens to be a huge empty room, shaped like a great hollow ball the size of a concert hall or a lesser sports stadium on Earth. It is used for all kinds of things, including ship systems, crew assemblies, competitions, and dances.

As a result, people get to dance inside the same room where they make the ship fly.

How is this possible?

The **interior surface** of the Resonance Chamber consists of **various layers of orichalcum** and other special materials that are exposed or covered as needed, to engage various functions. Like an onion, there are many layers that can be pulled back. Each layer is sensitive to sound in a different way, connected to various specific ship systems, and **acoustically** *isolated* from the others. When the Resonance Chamber is set a certain way, it is perfectly safe to go inside it and do all kinds of things, including physical training and dancing.

During her journey to Atlantis, Gwen goes to all the Zero-G dances but one—Green. However, she gets the chance to go to a Green Dance after all, a bittersweet occasion on the eve of their final mission to save Atlantis and Earth from the aliens. This Dance is held in orbit, inside the immense Resonance Chamber of the Atlantis Space Station, and is attended by Gwen, Aeson, their family and friends, and all the Fleet preparing to go into battle.

This, in itself, is an ancient Atlantean tradition—to celebrate hard before battle.

Why a *Green* Dance, and not some other color? Because the color of the Zero-G Dance theme is determined by the Quadrant *affiliation* **of the** *host*. In this case, the host is not a particular Quadrant *group*, but a *person*—the Atlantis Station Nomarch Evandros, and he belongs to the Green Quadrant.

CHAPTER 3 – Religion and Worldview

On Atlantis, religious beliefs and faith are just as varied as they are on Earth. However, there are no huge major religions that fight for political power while attempting to control behavior based on their moral code and norms across the general population. Instead, there are only many localized smaller belief sects and structures, carried over from ancient Earth with its numerous smaller deities worshipped regionally.

Faiths cross national borders in most cases and are low-key celebrations of daily life and existence. Add to this the **Cult of the Kassiopei Dynasty** and some very specific others, and you get a varied tapestry of belief and moral understanding. This includes forms of monotheism (a belief in one supreme god), polytheism (a belief in multiple gods), atheism, and agnosticism.

There are priesthoods dedicated to a variety of religions in both Imperial *Atlantida* and abroad. For example, the books introduce the reader to the **Priesthood of Kassiopei** and the **Priesthood of Amrevet-Ra**, the deity of Love, Union, and Matrimony. There are many others, such as **Mafdet**, the goddess of Law, Justice, and Retribution, for whom the "Needle of Justice" military solo fighter ship is named, or **Tyawu**, the god of Steady Winds and Fortune.

In general, Atlanteans have an *open-minded worldview* of the cosmos and of religious and spiritual beliefs, having come from Earth carrying a variety of diverse personal beliefs and traditions with them, stemming from the old days of the original colony. In addition, since they **needed to co-exist** with each other throughout the excruciating process of a difficult space journey and planetary colonization, Atlanteans learned not to impose their religious and cultural beliefs on others.

There are many faiths and religions on Atlantis, old gods and new ones, so their world is both *secular* and *faith-based*. Atlanteans have advanced science and technology—have had it for ages—and it does not interfere with their theological and faith-based interpretations of the universe. They have learned how to **reconcile**

both by understanding that science and religion are two aspects of the same reality, two faces of the same coin, two *methods* of analyzing existence.

As a result, some traditions are steeped in ancient beliefs and others are steeped in common sense. Same thing with the holidays— most **Atlantean holidays** have secular and religious aspects. And not everyone believes everything, or even the same thing. See *CHAPTER 8 – Calendar Holidays, Dates, Seasons* to learn more about the holidays.

While a certain part of the population worships the Imperial Family Kassiopei as gods (similar to how Ancient Egyptians *later* came to worship their pharaohs), it does not interfere with other faiths, cults, and denominations having their own share of life in society.

Furthermore, new faiths and beliefs on Atlantis are constantly arising and evolving. As Earth refugees integrate into Atlantean society, they bring all the contemporary Earth religions with them, so this new influx of belief will enrich Atlantean society in the long run.

Gwen herself is called a "Gebi Goddess" after her Logos voice powers variously reveal themselves, so that's already a cult in the making. And now that she can wield Starlight, things can get very interesting indeed.

Death and the Afterlife, Precursor to Ancient Egypt

The reader first begins to learn about Atlantean funeral and death customs on the ark-ships, in **Compete** (Chapter 21) when they burn the dead in ship incinerators in order to prevent the spread of infection after the terrorist uprising.

Gwen asks Aeson why they don't simply jettison the bodies into space. His reply is both practical and spiritual, a good example of the combined secular and faith-based worldview.

> *"We consider it disrespectful to the dead. It is also not very safe, especially not while we are in the Quantum Stream."*

And then he elaborates that **instead of prayers** said over the dead there are *songs*.

> *"On Atlantis we say goodbye to the dead by singing them onward to the great mystery of whatever comes next."*

Singing the dead onward is done at every funeral, as the gathered mourners raise their voices in unison and in harmony, to honor the departed and to make way for them in the great mystery beyond.

The Soul Triumvirate Afterlife Creed

Grief among the followers of the **oldest traditional afterlife creed** on Atlantis is expressed by the Imperatris Devora Kassiopei.

The **Soul Triumvirate Afterlife Creed** is not precisely a religion unto itself but a specific set of beliefs related *only* to what happens after death, and it does not interfere with an individual's other religious beliefs or affiliations with one deity or another.

In short, it is the belief that a sentient being has a **soul** consisting of three main parts—the *ka*, the *ba*, and the *akh*. The *ka* is the immortal life force, the aspect that is divine. The *ba* is the individuality—the specific person, colored, tainted and shaped by the life experiences in the physical world. The *akh* is the complete being reunited with all its soul parts in the afterlife.

When a person dies, the *ka* flees the physical body, forcing the *ba* to leave also, and they reunite on the other side to form the *akh*.

When a living person is grieving for the loss of a loved one, the survivor constantly experiences a "pull" or "tug" from the beyond, as the soul attempts to reunite with its beloved.

Devora Kassiopei describes grief as follows:

> *"Your heart is plunged in death's shadow, and your spirit is fractured prematurely. Your **ka** is poised between this world and the next, its life purpose faltering, while the **ba** is ready to flee on shadow*

*wings and take the **ka** with it. . . . And it must be agony because, for all practical purposes, the **akh** is already gone, having reunited with your beloved mate on the beyond side, the next stage of your mutual journey.*

"Grace is required for proper understanding. It is the nature of our human grief to best respond to the sublime, even as the grieving heart longs to regain clarity. . . . When we lose loved ones to death—ahead of ourselves—we rely on them to light the way first, as they travel ahead of us into the eternal realm. Then, for the rest of our lives, we are pulled relentlessly toward them by all the three parts of our spirit caught in that light. . . . Our physical bodies become limp, useless dolls controlled only by grief's far-reaching strings— especially in the beginning.

*"It is this fracturing into three that causes the imbalance that you are feeling now. As our three-layered spirit fabric is temporarily redefined, the new version of our selves has to be inscribed in **The Book of the Dead**. Once it is done, grief becomes bearable and life purpose returns. But—it takes time. Afterwards, of course, we are no longer the same in this world, because our loved one has taken parts of us, permanently.*

*"You are entangled with your love, and she is holding your **akh** in a safe embrace until your time comes."*

It is apparent that the Atlantean concept of the soul is the precursor to the Ancient Egyptian concepts, which expand and evolve on Earth after the Atlanteans are already gone.

CHAPTER 4 – The Kassiopei Dynasty

The **Kassiopei** Imperial Family is not merely the **oldest royal Dynasty** in existence but its members happen to possess the **oldest human DNA** known to humankind. This is not an exaggeration.

As the aliens of golden light explain at the end of **Survive**, the Kassiopei are in fact the descendants of the original humans created by some *other* yet-unknown, mysterious alien entity that may or may not be divine.

What is the origin of the Kassiopei bloodline? Are they truly divine? Were they made as gods to rule and to be worshipped?

The Kassiopei are in fact *not* gods. They are made as *servants*—strong, resilient, and virile. They are the earliest, healthiest, most robust of their kind, their DNA engineered to reinforce and maintain the **genetic integrity** of humanity's then-unstable young species on Earth.

Originally, the Kassiopei were created to be priests—to serve the spirit of all the living with the Logos voice of creation, and to *service* the early population with *their body*.

Instead, very soon after being created (by whatever mysterious means and whatever mysterious entity), the earliest Kassiopei choose to set themselves apart. They refuse to perform the responsibilities given to them and begin to acquire power for themselves and bestow controlled amounts of their genetic material to a limited number of chosen individuals.

They claim the Logos voice for their own, despite the fact that it belongs to all, and *anyone* can summon the inner resources to wield it—if the need and the focus is strong enough. Over time, the Kassiopei increasingly hoard power while minimizing interaction with other people to such an extent that their duty transforms into an elite ritual. By the time the *"They"* aliens return to Earth more than twelve thousand years ago, the Kassiopei are no longer humble priests serving at the disposal of their people, they now rule the entire population with an iron fist.

As time passes, the Imperial Kassiopei Dynasty takes on more and more esoteric power and significance in the eyes and imagination of their subject population. Their ability to wield the Logos voice seems to set them apart from others, its origin hidden in the murk of ages. The secret rituals they are rumored to be conducting on a regular basis are interpreted by the public as "magical" activities. And magic turns into godhood.

A priesthood arises to serve them in turn—assisting them with their greatly reduced original duties of procreation (the physical act of giving their genetic material to the population at large). They hoard the true knowledge about the purpose and details of the Rites of Sacrifice, keeping impeccable records of the progeny and persons involved in each generation, and perpetuating the cult of Kassiopei. They become known as the **Hel-Ra Priests**, or the **priests of Kassiopei**.

At the time of the original Ancient Atlantis on Earth, the Kassiopei are firmly established as *absolute rulers*, with nothing and no one—no advisory council or equal governing body—to balance and offset their imposition of power. It is only after they flee Earth and its apocalypse, that their absolute power starts to be limited by others. With the passing of millennia on the colony planet Atlantis, the system of government evolves to include a more democratic rule, and the **Imperial Executive Council** is established and gains in power.

By the time Etamharat Kassiopei and his son Romhutat are in power, the modern Imperator's powers are limited to a single IEC council vote, and any other unofficial influence is wielded only by financial or indirect means.

However, the *Kassiopeion*, a **temple** consecrated to the cult of the Imperial Kassiopei Dynasty, is maintained on the Palace complex premises, as a testament of their overwhelming influence. The looming building takes up much of the skyline in one area of the Imperial Palace complex. It is one of the tallest structures on these grounds, long and rectangular, with one narrow end incorporating a raised section with elements of a ziggurat tower and a flat-top pyramid. Like the Kassiopei, it is eternal.

Aeson
Kass

February
23, 2018
Vera Nazarian

Kassiopei Physical Traits and Differences

As mentioned earlier, the Kassiopei are strong, healthy, resilient, virile, and robust. It usually takes a Kassiopei male just **one sexual encounter** to impregnate his female partner, regardless of her ovulation cycle, because the Kassiopei sperm lives much longer and can "stick around" until the time is right.

And in order to avoid pregnancy, the female partner must take a special Kassiopei-only contraceptive on a regular basis (in the form of a drink).

When a child is born to a Kassiopei parent, they carry with them the full set of these unique genetic traits.

However, the outward physical features *may* or *may not* **manifest** unless a special **Bloodline Recognition Rite** is performed soon after conception and then repeated after birth by the parents. This ensures that the traits are fully expressed—and also provides visual proof for the Imperial Family and the public that the child is indeed Kassiopei.

The **Bloodline Recognition Rite** is a ritual to express the Kassiopei bloodline traits. It involves the *singing* of special voice commands by *both* the parents in unison, while embracing, and must be done soon after *conception*. Then, after the child is born, the ritual must be repeated, this time while holding the newborn, at least three times throughout the first week.

The two most **famous physical traits** of the Kassiopei are the *wedjat* **eyes** and the **golden hair**. The *wedjat* eye is a fine, sharp line of natural black pigment that outlines the edge of each eyelid, and is reminiscent of cosmetic eyeliner. The Kassiopei hair color is a unique pale blond shade with a gilded tint and faint metallic sheen that makes it appear like true gold, especially under bright illumination.

In Imperial *Atlantida*, one of the most long-standing manifestations of the cult of Kassiopei is the **fashion trend** among the general population to **dye their hair gold** and **outline their eyes with kohl** to mimic the Kassiopei divine rulers. It's a sign of respect with some and true reverent worship with the others.

When and how did this practice originate? One theory is that it came about as a side effect of the most ancient **Rite of Sacrifice**, when the ten annual Sacrificed noblewomen and their families assumed their obligatory exile from Court and Poseidon into provincial obscurity. When their next children were born (regardless of whether or not they were the actual Chosen family that year, or merely the other nine "decoys"), they all agreed to camouflage their children's appearance (and their own) by painting their hair and applying eyeliner as a "disguise" for the whole family, starting from an early age. This way, it would be hard to determine if their child really was a manifested Kassiopei offspring or if their appearance was merely a fashion statement expressing loyalty to the Throne. It is also assumed that the Kassiopei priesthood had a strong hand in directing the Sacrificed to engage in this practice.

Aeson explains it this way to Gwen in **Win**:

> *"It's easy to overlook something if you're not looking for it already. My children are being brought up in anonymity. Even if they somehow manifested the **wedjat** eyes and the natural golden hair, it would be mistaken for makeup. Remember, we Kassiopei might look a certain way, but so does the majority of the population. It's a popular custom to paint the eyelids and the hair to mimic the Imperial Family. For generations it's been encouraged as a semi-religious practice. But secretly, in reality, it's yet another Rite-related*

> *practice intended to disguise the Sacrificed, to*
> *preserve the anonymity of the illegitimate*
> *Kassiopei in the general population."*

Other less visible but more important Kassiopei traits include an unusual **sexual stamina**, and related to it (because of a nearly perfect balance of hormones and more efficient absorption of nutrients) **immunity** to many diseases and adverse environmental factors including the detrimental effects of the Quantum Jump technology.

The Rite of Sacrifice

All unmarried Kassiopei males between the ages of sixteen and nineteen are required to participate in an annual rite that has been their duty since the dawn of time. This primarily involves Crown Prince Heirs, but occasionally applies to their brothers, uncles, and any other living Kassiopei male relatives that might fit the age and special criteria. The latter circumstances are less common, but have been known to occur over the centuries.

Once they come of age (sixteen Atlantean years, the equivalent of twenty and a half Earth years), the young men are obligated by law to perform their Imperial Kassiopei duty once a year, and they are only relieved of this obligation if they find a wife by the age of nineteen (a strong incentive to marry, for Heirs in particular). Otherwise, they must perform the duty indefinitely.

The Imperial Rite of Sacrifice requires for the Kassiopei male to be *physically intimate* with several specially chosen, verifiably *fertile* women of nobility, in a highly controlled, completely **anonymous coupling ritual** for the duration of one night. It is overseen by the Kassiopei priests (also known as Hel-Ra priests), and to some degree, several members of the Imperial Family. The Rite is explained in **Win**, Chapter 23.

One might ask, **why**, with all the Atlantean advanced technology, **is this archaic ritual still necessary?** Doesn't Atlantis have high-tech science and more clinical ways of extracting the DNA without resorting to primitive physical means that might have been played out in Ancient Egypt?

The following explanation comes from the priests of Kassiopei. Yes, modern science has the means of extracting DNA in a clinical setting. But there's at least one very practical reason for having the Rite.

Due to the very nature of their enhanced DNA, all Kassiopei males have unusually powerful physical urges. They are driven to express their genetic potential, yet they must remain **highly controlled** when it comes to **sexual intimacy**. They are required to abstain from sex outside of marriage. And their physical needs become unbearable. The Rite serves to alleviate some of this, and it has been this way for thousands of years.

The Talk with the Imperatris

Gwen learns that if she and Aeson are to make love, even once, without using any protection, she would become pregnant. The probability is almost one hundred percent.

For some time, she has no idea if there's anything that can be done to prevent it. And then she has *the talk* with Aeson's mother, Devora, as described in **Survive**, Chapter 50.

Devora Kassiopei explains to her gently, over a cup of *aeojir*, what to expect on her Wedding Night. According to the Imperatris (who had a similar talk with the previous Imperatris before her), the Kassiopei men have an overwhelming physical drive, and at the same time, they are incredibly fertile. However, the Imperial Wife has a choice in regard to pregnancy by taking the proper precaution—a special contraceptive drink right before the *Amrevet* Night.

Additionally, the Imperatris shares other embarrassing details of intimacy. During the *act*, Kassiopei males *finish quickly*. Sometimes, before their partner does. However, they have almost **no rest period** and are ready to perform once more almost immediately.

> *"In short, you will have no interruption to your own physical fulfillment. The Kassiopei man will have you very well satisfied at the end of your night."*

CHAPTER 5 – Imperial Court

The Imperial Court structure of Ancient Atlantis and the colony planet's oldest nation Imperial *Atlantida* have evolved and cultivated three divisions of power and prestige: **Low Court**, **Middle Court**, and **High Court**. These divisions are entirely based on the number of generations that any given family has held the rank of nobility over the years—and in most cases, over the centuries.

Imperial Court of *Atlantida*

High Court – Noble Houses of at least 50 generations of nobility.

Middle Court – Noble Houses of at least 20 to 49 generations of nobility.

Low Court – Noble Houses of at least 1 to 19 generations of nobility.

Below is an example of a proper Courtly self-introduction (Xelio's mother, presenting herself to the Imperial Bride during Gwen's Ladies of the Court Bridal event):

> *"First Lady Aduar Vekahat, of the House Vekahat, of the Southern Uru Province, one hundred and ninth generation, High Court."*

The designation "First Lady" indicates that she is the highest-ranking female of her House.

Imperial Court Functions

The Imperator holds Court at the Imperial Palace, in the form of Assemblies, Receptions, and other formal functions. The most resplendent venue is the Imperial Throne Hall called the **Pharikoneon**—the ancient grand chamber dedicated to the highest Imperial ceremonies.

The floor of the *Pharikoneon* is colored in **three sections**, on both sides of the central red path leading up to the throne. Closest to the throne, the floor tiles are pale stone, almost white. That is the High Court. Only the highest nobility is permitted to stand there. Then comes a section of stone floor in red—a divider—followed by an area in golden cream yellow—that is the Middle Court. Next, another divider in red, and at last, the section in rust orange, toward the back of the chamber. It is the Low Court.

Once the Court is assembled, and the Imperator opens the **Imperial Court Session**, the red path to the throne and the red sections on the floor may not be tread upon by anyone who is not of Imperial blood, unless the Imperator or another member of the Imperial Family grants them permission. Everyone else must stand on the floor in their designated section, and may not step on any red tile.

The distant wall behind the thrones is pure gold, with an intricate sunburst relief which is the Ra symbol—the sun symbol of the Kassiopei Dynasty.

The huge **throne** is a tall-backed golden chair, upraised on a dais of five steps. To the right of it is a lesser gold chair, and to the left, another, both intended for other members of the Imperial Family. Backless gold benches complete the lineup on both sides, for yet other relatives or those who are favored by the Imperator. The entire section is called the **Imperial Seats**.

Other functions are held in lesser chambers, or in other buildings on the grounds of the Imperial Palace complex.

Court Attire

In order to attend an Imperial Assembly or any other Court function, Atlanteans must be splendidly dressed. Their formal outfits are amazing in all the three sections of Court. And yet, there's a marked difference between delicate Low Court garb—a few well-placed pieces of jewelry, simple flow of hair, and the austere fall of elegantly understated dress fabric—and High Court ladies in wildly intricate headdresses, with upswept sculpted hair, dramatic makeup, sparkling webs and garlands of jewelry and dresses of so many layers that they are like sculptures in themselves.

The men are predominantly capped with grand golden wigs in all three sections, with the same differences in levels of complexity, from austere to extravagant. They also wear amazing layers of makeup, perfectly fitted jackets and pants or floor-length robes and capes.

To an untrained eye, the fine distinctions between Middle Court and High Court blur. However, there is a level of complexity and opulence in High Court attire that Middle Court cannot match. Middle Court fashions are resplendent but not outlandish. The term that best describes the High Court look is *ridiculous luxury*.

CHAPTER 6 – Foods of The Atlantis Grail

Friendly warning! The foods and mealtimes mentioned in the series are liable to make you very hungry, according to many readers (and prompt you to visit the refrigerator—so sorry, the author says guiltily).

Whether lingering at early morning *eos* bread, formal afternoon *dea* meals, having an intimate *niktos* meal with family and dear friends, or even a midnight ghost meal, the characters seem to spend a lot of time eating. Supposedly, food relaxes and brings out the truth in relationships. Some of the best discussions and revelations happen over this ritual of taking in sustenance and spilling one's soul to someone you love. And so do some of the best plot twists. . . .

An Atlantean day, being 27 hours long, gives plenty of time to eat *four* regular meals instead of merely three:

1. ***Eos* bread** – the equivalent of Earth breakfast.
2. ***Dea* meal** – the equivalent of late lunch.
3. ***Niktos* meal** – the equivalent of late dinner.
4. **Ghost meal** – eaten around midnight, a light meal featuring snacks and comfort food.

Atlantis has some unusual eating customs. Atlanteans do not have a dining room or dedicated eating area in the home. Instead, their food is brought to them wherever they happen to be, a kind of personal food service. Food cooking and serving stations are set up, and dishes are prepared right there to order, indulging all your preferences. If needed, temporary tables are unfolded, and food is served there.

Naturally this applies to privileged classes—nobility, citizens, and the wealthy who can afford to keep a personal cooking staff. Ordinary civilian commoners serve themselves and their families in whatever room or living area everyone is gathered.

Vegan and Vegetarian Lifestyle

Modern Atlanteans adhere to a primarily vegan and vegetarian lifestyle, for complex social, ethical, and health reasons that are touched upon in the core series, especially **Survive**, and are explored in greater depth in the prequel series, *Dawn of the Atlantis Grail.*

The reasons for this lifestyle are ancient and multifaceted, and date to a period over 12,500 years ago, just before the fall of the original continent Atlantis on Earth with the arrival of *"They,"* the unnamed, mysterious aliens who are welcomed as gods by the majority of the less advanced ancient world (Ancient Egypt and Mesopotamia, in particular), However, the technologically advanced Ancient Atlanteans recognize the aliens as merely superior beings.

In the process of first contact with the ruling elites of the continent Atlantis (but not first contact with Earth, according to the aliens themselves who claim to have visited humanity's home planet several times earlier throughout the ages) and resulting negotiations, the aliens make a **twofold ultimatum** to Atlanteans: close their recently opened and highly unstable dimensional rift, and stop eating and abusing other animal species, or be destroyed.

Closing the dangerous rift makes immediate sense, but why a vegan mandate? The ultimatum as a whole was intended as a complete *species reset*—to return humanity to their original status of benevolent sentient protectors instead of selfish abusers. This is the same core notion of humankind as "stewards of creation" that was *later* described in Biblical texts.

In addition, this was a cleansing reversion to a purified original state before humanity picked up their bad habits—the so-called "Fall." This and other ancient concepts are explained in the prequel series, and the mysteries of ancient Earth religions and their sociological implications brought to light.

Given a ridiculously brief span of only five years to make radical changes to their society, the Atlanteans (and by example the rest of the ancient peoples of Earth) are suddenly compelled to take on a vegan lifestyle—on pain of annihilation. Naturally, this mandate is not easy to enact over an entire population used to consuming meat and animal products, especially the lower classes and the poor who have limited or no choice in their form of sustenance.

"Man, I missed Shesep's Bar!"

—Anu Vei

While the privileged classes experiment with sophisticated recipes for delicious plant-based proteins and high-end healthy nutrition, the poor are left to fend for themselves with what they can find and forage. There are harsh laws passed and correctors sent to enforce them. The less privileged suffer the brunt of those strict, new dietary laws.

In those transitional years on Earth there are many overlooked infractions in the beginning. The poorest commoners resort to secretly consuming meat and, in particular, fish in coastal areas. The habit of seafood consumption is nearly impossible to eradicate, and it only stops completely when the Atlanteans are forced by necessity to limit their diet while on board their ancient Fleet of ships escaping Earth and its ancient asteroid apocalypse.

However, once they arrive on the colony planet Atlantis, and the population spreads across the landmass with its plentiful natural resources, seafood consumption resurfaces in the most remote, wild areas, away from cities and hubs of ruling power and their law enforcement.

But by then the most privileged elites have gotten used to the strictly vegan lifestyle and experience the health benefits, especially considering the emergence of the Long Illness that affects the oldest and youngest among them (caused by the multiple Quantum Jumps).

"You smell like the eastern wharf at low tide. And moldy scarab beer!"

—Gennio Rukkat

The middle and lower classes are less strict and are primarily vegetarian, using some animal products such as dairy and honey, but not consuming the animals themselves. And the most impoverished population are desperate to consume any protein they can get, especially the barren coastal villages where the sea provides their only source of sustenance.

With time, the idea of eating fish becomes an insult (see *CHAPTER 16 – Atlanteo Language Glossary* for the various insult terms), and is looked down upon as a filthy practice and a symptom of lower status (in addition to animal cruelty ethical concerns).

And this perpetuates over the centuries to the modern day Atlantean diet lifestyle—a combination of ethics, health, status, and ancient tradition, in a complex gradation from strict vegan to borderline vegetarian.

Fun Fact: Establishments such as Shesep's Bar in Fish Town must obtain special licensing in order to serve various seafood entrees.

The Ethics of Not Eating Animals

The complex ethics of not eating animals are effectively presented by Princess Manala during their time at Shesep's Bar in Fish Town.

Manala tells Gwen that the sea creatures and all the living creatures thank her *so much* for not eating them. Gwen jokingly asks her, what about the vegetables?

But Manala responds:

> *"The vegetables are alive, but they are not creatures. They live in a different phase of being, out of sync with us—like the pegasei. When we reach across phases of being to take energy, we cause the least harm. It is only when we rob others similar to ourselves of energy that we do wrong."*

Gwen is not quite sure what to make of this, so she merely smiles at her.

"What if people on Earth were suddenly told to set all their cows free because they are in fact sentient aliens? Cattle ranchers would riot. It would be World War Three—no, Three and a Half, since there's already World War Three: Asteroid Edition, happening now."

—George Lark

Foods of TAG

Below is a comprehensive list of **every edible item** mentioned in the books, presented in no particular order except its appearance in the series, and listed under the corresponding meal times when it was being consumed. The Earth food items, mentioned primarily in **Qualify**, are included for the completists.

Earth

 Drinks:

Apple juice
Coffee
Fruit punch
Ginger Ale
Milk
Orange juice

Breakfast:

Cheesy garlic eggs
Hash browns
Pancakes with maple syrup

Entrees:

Burgers
Greasy macaroni casserole
Pizza
Chili dogs
Meatloaf
Spaghetti
Roast beef hot sandwich
Italian Salami
Bologna
Trout / *Ishkhan* (Armenian) / *Farel* (Russian)

Sides:

French fries
Cole slaw
Mashed potatoes

Fresh veggies
Corn
Cheesy fries

 *Desserts:*

Jello
Cherry pie
Ice cream cone
Yogurt
White cake with frosting
Cookies

Atlantis

 Drinks:

Nikkari **juice** – thick algae-greenish liquid that tastes like watermelon ambrosia.

Lvikao – hot, invigorating drink that smells like pastries in a bakery, has some caffeine, and is comparable to Earth coffee blended with cocoa and spices: "Creamy notes of what could be vanilla bean, saffron, nutmeg, marzipan, cinnamon, hazelnut, bitter chocolate, and other unknown alien delicacies create a complex bouquet of flavor."

Qvaali – mildly alcoholic beverage that is dark plum-colored, foams, smells like hops, wheat, and raspberries, and tastes like apple cider with a hint of berries and wheat. *(The drink was inspired by traditional Russian Kvass, a fermented beverage made from black rye bread, admits the author, who happens to love the stuff.)*

Scarab beer – dark brown ale. Traditional Atlantean version is a specialty that is made from harvested scarabs that died a natural death (hence, cruelty-free), then aged and dried with their internal organs (and dung) intact for a month, then ground and mixed with the liquid for the beer.

Aeojir – light brew of pleasantly fragrant plant leaves steeped in hot water that has a rich, amber color. This is the Atlantean equivalent of tea. The plant used is native to the colony planet Atlantis, but similar to Earth's *camellia sinensis.*

Protein drink that tastes like a pineapple and citrus punch. Unnamed drink given to Gwen after her pre-wedding day of fasting.

Shedehur – strong alcoholic beverage similar to red wine that is a persimmon-amber color and smells like crisp apples. It was served at the Wedding reception.

 *Eos Bread:*

Mixed fruit and vegetable scramble – a dish combining a variety of fruits and vegetables from both Earth and Atlantis that tastes vaguely like an egg scramble that includes tomatoes, mushrooms, and zucchini. One of the first full meals served to the newly-Qualified Earth refugees on board the ark-ships, a true fusion of Earth and Atlantean ingredients in an effort to acclimate the Earthies to alien shipboard food.

Savory dumplings with or without creamy sauce.

Pancake-like edibles covered in sweet honey-sauce and sprinkled with fruit.

Aromatic baked **pastry rolls**.

Eos **pie** – a popular morning dish, similar to a hand pie. Can be either sweet or savory.

Medoi fruit-filled *eos* **pie** – described as a "big, juicy, swirly, fruity thing."

Pseudo-donut pastries – also known as *ecurami*.

Sweet **drenched fruit** and a **savory dish of flaky pastry** aromatic with spices.

Buttery dumplings sprinkled with spicy and crunchy bits that taste like hickory-smoked nuts

Savory *durzaio* – buttered rolls.

Mashed *djebabat* with thick dollops of **spicy gravy** – Atlantean comfort food, similar to mashed potatoes.

✦ *Dea or Niktos Meal Entrees:*

Savory *lidairi* **and** *ero* **grains stir fry** – Aeson's favorite simple dish.

Varoite – sweet-sour-savory noodle-like dish with pungent greens.

Baidao **stew** – similar to chunky vegetable stew.

Rigavi **rolls** – bread rolls reminiscent of Earth dinner rolls, plain or stuffed like piroshki.

Crispy waffle "thing" that's colored orange with streaks of green.

Various spicy and savory dishes with herbs, reminiscent of Mediterranean Food.

Layered *gulubo* **in cream sauce** – sprinkled with savory herbs and/or sweet candied drizzle of fruit; a cross between flaky pastry and lasagna, with many layers of delicious vegetable and/or fruit fillings.

Syrup-drenched dumpling – a dough pocket with a wide variety of either savory or sweet fillings, can be eaten during any meal, with recipes ranging from high cuisine to common comfort food.

✦ *Dea or Niktos Meal Side Dishes or Buffet Items:*

Vegetables with or without creamy sauces, tasting of smoky rich pungency, with pleasant textures and savory flavors.

Savory aromatic **stir-fried vegetables**.

Seasonal fruit and pastry sculpture gallery – a three-dimensional artful food structure presented at feasts, served on top of long buffet tables. It often includes "rivers" of drink circulating via fountain pumps flowing around "mountains" constructed from individual pastries. Often seen at Court functions, at the Imperial Palace.

Fried root vegetables and pickled *ranub* – a dish reminiscent of vegetarian antipasto, consisting of a platter with brined and pickled vegetables combined with grilled or fried ones.

Ozu **butter** – a buttery dipping sauce, with a savory, "garlicky" oil base flavored with smoked herbs and spices.

Various savory **flatbreads** – similar to Indian naan, Armenian lavash, and other Middle Eastern flatbreads.

Multi-layered **deep-dish delicacy baked in flaky pastry dough** and topped with a savory herb crust – a layered dish in the same style as *gulubo*.

Fragrant **vegetable cream soup inside shallow bowls** of sculpted dough blossoms – reminiscent of Earth bread bowl thick soups and dips served inside hollowed out loaves of crusty bread.

 *Non-Vegetarian Seafood Entrees and Sides:*

Grilled *sukrat* – saltwater fish with a strong flavor.

Spicy *guu* **rolls** – similar to Earth sushi rolls, but the fish is cooked, not raw.

Maqooi **fish eggs on flatbread** – Atlantean version of caviar on blini (Russian thin pancake, or crepe).

Makuuda **filet** – fish that is mild and savory with a hint of sweetness.

Shelled *kivakat* – Atlantean shellfish considered a local delicacy in Fish Town (Golden Bay).

Ghost Meal or Snacks:

Savory pastry stuffed with spicy vegetables.

Edible **nuggets of baked dough** similar to Earth potato chips.

Savory noodles in thick, plum-colored sauce.

Fruit and nuts drenched in aromatic syrup.

Hurucaz – small, grape-like fruit with a tart flavor.

Cheburi pie – savory pie filled with spicy plant-based protein, like an Earth meat pie, but vegan.

Desserts:

Cobbler with strange great violet berries that smell like honeydew and caramel.

Puff pastry drenched in creamy sauce and sprinkled with native nuts that taste like Earth hazelnuts.

Sweet, cold dessert that is vaguely similar to honey ice cream.

Biuo – large exotic red-and-green fruit that looks like a striated prickly apple.

Bowl of orange-colored **tart fruit in sweet sauce**.

Ecurami – impossibly delicious dessert puffs filled with creamy goodness that Gordie discovered at his workplace. *Ecurami* is a local specialty that's supposedly flash-baked in special ultra-hot ovens and sold only in the food court of the Heri Agriculture HQ industrial complex where he works. Also described as pseudo-donuts when sold elsewhere in Poseidon.

Amrevet **pies** – shaped like four-point stars, made on special nuptial occasions, such as the Imperial Wedding.

Ihamar – airy, frozen fruit delight similar to ice cream, but with the ephemeral texture of snow, meringue, and powdered sugar placed on top of paper-thin sliced of melon-colored fruit—where they quiver with so much as a breath—and then drizzled in a delicate, violet syrup with an aroma of rose petals. As the syrup flows, it creates deep crystalline gullies and paints a delightful, abstract picture. An Imperial Court delicacy.

Fuchmik – a dry, barely sweet, dessert stick made in the city of Khur in Shuria. (It was inspired by a beloved sweet treat from the author's childhood, *Churchkhela*, a traditional dessert in the Republic of Georgia. Each Churchkhela is shaped like a long candle, its "wick" a string threaded with nuts which are then dipped multiple times in grape paste thickened with flour, and sometimes other fruit syrup concentrate, and hung to dry in the sun for several days. No sugar is added, so it is pleasantly barely sweet, never cloying, and makes a filling, high calorie trail snack. In Armenia it is known as *kaghtsr sujukh*.)

Fun Fact: Rejoice, foodies, there will be an Atlantis Grail Cookbook!

CHAPTER 7 – Geography and Places

Locations play an important role in the series, ranging from Earth and the solar system, to Atlantis and its moons, the Helios planetary system, and the farthest reaches of deep space and the greater universe beyond.

Earth

The story begins in northwestern Vermont, in **Highgate Waters**, an imaginary small town near the very real St. Albans, the current residence of the Lark family, and the local high school. From there, the action moves to **Pennsylvania** and the Regional Qualification Center (RQC-3).

Next, the Semi-Finals take us to **Los Angeles, California** for the grueling urban race from a hillside somewhere near Glendora and on for thirty miles toward the city center at the heart of downtown.

Gwen's Los Angeles Itinerary
(Sort of, from Author's Original Silly Notes)

Glendora → Azusa → Duarte → Arcadia → San Marino (Huntington Gardens) → South Pasadena → Alhambra → Montecito Heights (cross the 5 Freeway) → Chinatown (cross the 101 Freeway) → Downtown

Along the way, there's a detour to the Huntington Library, Art Museum, and Botanical Gardens, a trek across the concrete basin of the L. A. River, and a journey through Skid Row.

After the Semi-Finals ordeal, the next destination is the United States National Qualification Center (NQC), located somewhere in the Eastern Plains of **Colorado.**

Finally, the Finals commence in the Atlantic Ocean, somewhere off-shore between Jacksonville, **Florida** and the Florida Keys—

which are flooded and completely submerged underwater at the time of the story.

The action continues from a sunken cave (one of many entry points to an Ancient Atlantean subterranean tunnel network) through the tunnels, spanning a distance of 1,000 miles underneath the ocean floor and culminating in the middle of the Atlantic Ocean right underneath Ancient Atlantis itself—the modern-day area spanning **Bermuda** and the **Bahamas**.

Finally, Earth is left behind as shuttles soar into the sky toward the great ark-ships in Earth's orbit.

The Coral Reef Cosmic Neighborhood

After a year-long journey through space in the general direction of the constellation of Pegasus (The Great Square) traversing the solar system, departing The Milky Way Galaxy, jumping an immeasurable distance across the universe, then entering an immeasurably distant **Galaxy** called **The Coral Reef**, the Earth refugees arrive in the **Helios system** neighborhood, home of the ancient colony planet Atlantis.

Unlike Earth—and its entire solar system, located on the outer edge of one of the spiral arms of the Milky Way Galaxy—Atlantis and the Hel solar system are in a very central spot in their galaxy, at the base of the spiral and somewhat off the galactic plane. It's why the Atlantis night sky is so dense with stars—trillions of stars, and rich layers of colors and nebulae. It's even possible to see the swirling arms of the spiral galaxy with the naked eye.

On Earth, all that's visible of its home galaxy is a distant faint trail—hence, the Milky Way. Earth and its sun are so far away from the galactic center, that there are fewer visible stars, and fewer objects in the sky in general, and the night sky looks black.

Meanwhile, The Coral Reef Galaxy—named for the reddish and rose colors of the largest visible nebula, and for the fact that coral reefs are alive, seething with color and vibrant energy—is a more spectacular sight, at least from Atlantis's vantage point.

However, being located so close to the center of the galaxy has its own major drawbacks and a terrible danger aspect. At the heart of The Coral Reef Galaxy lies an immense **black hole** called **Ae-Leiterra**.

"What kind of *shar-ta-haak shebet* is going on there?"

—Xelio Vekahat

It is an *active galactic nucleus*, so that a whole lot of brightness is visible at an immense distance. That's the exterior of the **Rim** of Ae-Leiterra. All the accretion disk matter is spinning so fast around the black hole that the plasma is being ejected in two powerful jets, in opposite directions—one from each axis pole—and flung outward into space. It is a deadly *quasar* pointed in a direction that barely "grazes" the area which contains Hel's system and Atlantis—which are raised off the flat galactic plane as they circle the center of the galaxy. It is not a direct strike but a sideways "swipe," creating sufficient proximity to the lethal radiation zone.

Normally, if the jets are pointing even remotely in your direction what you get is deadly radiation and super brightness, and at such proximity there is no habitable zone. Under any other circumstances Atlantis would be fried to a crisp together with all other Hel's planets, and Hel itself. But luckily, there is an immense **Black Nebula** blocking the fury of the jets in that exact spot, wonderfully located between Hel's system and the deadly inferno.

The Black Nebula is an immense, long, cosmic **string-filament structure**, shaped like a worm, with its one end facing Atlantis and the other end being side-swipe-bombarded by the Ae-Leiterra quasar. The nebula consists of hot, non-radiant matter and gas—nothing but microscopic matter for light years in that direction—creating a safety dust curtain between Hel's system and radiation hell. The Ae-Leiterra quasar is spewing, but the Black Nebula just happens to be in its path.

Since the Black Nebula obscures most of Ae-Leiterra, it shields Atlantis and makes life and survival possible in the Helios system despite its relative proximity to the active galactic center. It creates a *miraculous habitable zone* in an otherwise deadly place in the galaxy.

Some people in the SPC "worship the blessed worm." Pilot patrols love the Black Nebula. It's considered good luck.

Despite the immense role it plays, the Black Nebula (and beyond it, Ae-Leiterra) appears only as a *small dark spot* in one part of the Atlantis sky. Among a thicket of stars, it's a small, vaguely circular area that's mostly black and devoid of light.

The Rim of Ae-Leiterra is the place where Aeson Kassiopei loses his life saving the entire Fleet. He is later miraculously resurrected, and earns the right to wear the black armband of a hero.

The Colony Planet Atlantis

Atlantis is a fertile and beautiful blue-green planet orbiting a bright, golden-white star **Helios** (commonly shortened to **Hel**). It is the fifth planet, has three moons (until a fourth, the Ghost Moon, is discovered), and is located in the habitable zone of its star system. The five inner planets (**Rah, Septu, Tammuz, Ishtar, Atlantis**) are rocky worlds, while the two outer planets (**Olympos, Atlas**) are gas giants.

Helios is a radiant white star, about 10% larger and 25% brighter than Earth's Sol. Hel's rocky planets in order of proximity to it are shown below.

Helios Planetary System

Helios	☼
Rah	○
Septu	○
Tammuz	○
Ishtar	○
Atlantis	○
Olympos	○
Atlas	○

Atlantis is a planet very similar to Earth, but slightly larger in circumference. From Earth's vantage point, it is located in the area of the sky that is known as the constellation of Pegasus, or the Great Square. Because the colony planet has slightly more mass, it exerts somewhat more gravity than Earth, which causes some initial problems for the human colonists as they get acclimated to it (and the extra weight).

The sun of Atlantis is slightly bigger and brighter than Earth's Sol, so daylight is more blazing, and the daytime sky appears white. The seasons are longer due to a longer orbit and therefore longer year. The Atlantean year is **417 Atlantean days** (the equivalent of approximately 469 Earth days. In his explanation during one of his classes at Pennsylvania RQC-3, Nefir Mekei reports it inaccurately as 417 *Earth* days.)

The day is slightly longer also, the equivalent of Earth's **27 hours**, because Atlantis rotates along its axis a bit slower than Earth.

It should be noted that the Earth and Atlantean equivalents of hour, minute, and second are so close in length that they can be considered the same. For example, there are 60 minutes in both Earth and Atlantean hours (with the exception of Ghost Times which are half-hour periods).

The atmosphere is oxygen rich, similar to Earth. There's somewhat less surface water on Atlantis, with only a single oceanic belt around the middle of the planet. It is divided (by nomenclature, not physical geography) into two large oceans, the **Djetatlan Ocean** and the **Nehehatlan Ocean**, that together cover approximately one half of the planet while the rest is mostly green forests and tall snow-covered mountains.

The planet is divided into two hemispheres, the **Upper Hemisphere** (also known as the *Lower Shadow Hemisphere*, since it is the "shadow" side from the vantage point of the Lower Hemisphere), and the **Lower Hemisphere** (also known as the *Upper Shadow Hemisphere*). The Upper Hemisphere contains Imperial *Atlantida* which occupies most of the large continental landmass that "descends" from the northern pole (**Pole of Ra**)—hence, the "upper." Meanwhile, the Lower Hemisphere contains New Deshret which occupies most of the large landmass that "rises" from the southern pole (**Pole of Khe**).

There is plenty of wildlife. However, unlike Earth, Atlantis is very sparsely populated with people. There are fewer than a billion human beings on the colony planet, and fewer than seventy national boundaries, with several main cities.

Places and Locations

The following places have been mentioned or described in the series.

Imperial *Atlantida:*

Poseidon, or City of Poseidon, the Capital of Imperial *Atlantida.*
Agnios Park (Poseidon)
Phoinios Heights (Poseidon)
Themisera, or Sky Tangle City (Poseidon)
Fish Town (Poseidon)
Koruut District (Poseidon)

Golden Bay of Poseidon (east and west of city center, and the entire gulf area)

Eastern Provinces along the Great Nacarat Plateau

Northern Sesemet Province (forests and flatlands)

Western Xeneret Province (forests and flatlands)

Northern Mithektet Province (agricultural)

Northeast Uotai Province

Southeast Raia Province

Agnios Coast

Southern Aravat Province

Eastern Vadat Province

Eastern Quzakat Province

Eastern Duinaat Province

Tatenen (city in Imperial *Atlantida*)

Benben Island (part of archipelago of seven tiny islands called the Akhet Islands or Horizon Islands, located off the coast of Poseidon, in the Golden Bay)

Bujug (small town in Uotai Province)

Defo (small town in Raia Province)

Vaioluth River (North of Great Nacarat Plateau)

Foreign Locations:

Dubutaat Mountain (New Deshret)

Xois (Capital city of New Deshret)

Khenneb

Nehehatlan Ocean

Djetatlan Ocean

Easter Egg: Can you find the "Chicken Sea" on the map?

Atlantean Countries

There are almost **seventy nations** on the colony planet Atlantis. Below is a list of the largest ones, as marked on the map. A few tiny ones have been marked by boundaries but not named on the map, so they are not listed.

Ab-Ur – Lower Hemisphere, part of Lower Continent. Shares borders with Seba, Ankh-Tawi, and one other state (unnamed), vassal of New Deshret.

Abuud – Lower Hemisphere, part of Upper Continent. Shares border with Hemet-Saret.

Ankh-Tawi – Lower Hemisphere, part of Lower Continent. Polar nation on the lower side, temperate cool climate on upper. Shares borders with New Deshret, Ab-Ur, Ptahleon, Bastet, Nuu, Weret, and three other states (unnamed). Vassal of New Deshret.

Bastet – Upper Hemisphere, part of Lower Continent. Polar nation. Shares borders with Ankh-Tawi, Ptahleon, and one other state (unnamed).

Chimir – Lower Hemisphere, part of Lower Continent. Shares border with and is a vassal of New Deshret.

Dea *(island)* – Upper Hemisphere, in Djetatlan Ocean, grouped with Lower Continent. Polar nation.

Eos-Heket – spans Upper and Lower Hemisphere, part of Upper Continent. Polar nation on upper side. Shares border with and is an ally of Imperial *Atlantida*. Also borders Iaat, Vai Naat, Xeosan, and three other states (unnamed).

Hemet-Saret – Lower Hemisphere, part of Upper Continent. Shares borders with Abuud, Vai Naat, and five other states (unnamed).

Iaat – Upper Hemisphere, part of Upper Continent. Shares borders with and is an ally of Eos-Heket and one other state (unnamed).

Ibek – spans Upper and Lower Hemisphere, part of Upper Continent. Shares borders with Maat and Rarek.

Imperial *Atlantida* – Upper Hemisphere, part of Upper Continent. Shares borders with and is an ally of Eos-Heket and Ubasti.

Kai-Pa – Upper Hemisphere, part of Upper Continent. Shares borders with and is an ally of Ubasti and four other states (unnamed).

Karamat – Upper Hemisphere, part of Upper Continent. Polar nation. Shares borders with and is an ally of Vai Naat, Xeosan, and one other state (unnamed).

Khenneb – Upper Hemisphere, part of Upper Continent. Shares borders with and is an ally of Ubasti. Also shares borders with Wefa, Seger, and Rarek.

Liant – Upper Hemisphere, part of Upper Continent. Shares border with Rarek.

Maat – spans Upper and Lower Hemisphere, part of Upper Continent. Shares borders with Seger, Ibek, and Rarek.

Mereva *(island)* – Upper Hemisphere, in Nehehatlan Ocean, grouped with Lower Continent, polar nation. Neighbor of Bastet.

Neb – Lower Hemisphere, part of Upper Continent. Shares border with its ally Qurartu.

New Deshret – Lower Hemisphere, part of Lower Continent. Shares borders with Weret, Ankh-Tawi, Chimir, Ptahleon and three other nations (unnamed), all its vassal states.

Nuu – Lower Hemisphere, part of Lower Continent. Polar nation. Shares borders with Ptahleon, Weret, and Ankh-Tawi. Vassal of New Deshret.

Ptahleon – spans Upper and Lower Hemisphere, part of Lower Continent. Polar nation. Shares border with and is an ally of Shuria, neighbor of Bastet.

Qurartu – Lower Hemisphere, part of Upper Continent. Shares borders with and is an ally of Ubasti, Neb, and another nation (unnamed).

Rarek – Upper Hemisphere, part of Upper Continent. Shares borders with Liant, Khenneb, Seger, Maat, and Ibek.

Seba – Lower Hemisphere, part of Lower Continent. Shares borders with Ab-Ur and three other states (unnamed), vassal of New Deshret.

Seger – spans Upper and Lower Hemisphere, part of Upper Continent. Shares borders with Khenneb, Wefa, Maat, and Rarek.

Semiras *(island archipelago)* – Lower Hemisphere, in Djetatlan Ocean, grouped with Lower Continent. Neighbor of Chimir, vassal of New Deshret.

Shuria – Upper Hemisphere, part of Lower Continent. Shares border with and is an ally of Ptahleon.

Ubasti – spans Upper and Lower Hemisphere, part of Upper Continent. Polar nation on upper side. Shares borders with and is an ally of Imperial *Atlantida*, Kai-Pa, Vai-Naat, Khenneb, Zinas,

Qurartu, and other small nations (unnamed). Also shares border with Wefa.

Vai Naat – spans Upper and Lower Hemisphere, part of Upper Continent. Polar nation. Shares borders with and is an ally of Eos-Heket, Ubasti, Zinas, and other small nations (unnamed). Ally of Imperial *Atlantida*.

Wefa – spans Upper and Lower Hemisphere, part of Upper Continent. Shares borders with Ubasti, Khenneb, and Seger.

Weret – Lower Hemisphere, part of Lower Continent. Polar nation on lower side. Shares borders with New Deshret, Nuu, Ankh-Tawi, Ptahleon, and one other nation (unnamed). Vassal of New Deshret.

Xeosan – Upper Hemisphere, part of Upper Continent. Polar nation. Shares borders with and is an ally of Vai Naat, Eos-Heket, and Karamat.

Zinas – Upper Hemisphere, part of Upper Continent. Polar nation. Shares borders with and is an ally of Ubasti, Vaiu Naat, and Eos-Heket.

Flora and Fauna of Atlantis

Animal species are abundant on Atlantis. During the original colony period, newly arrived Ancient Atlanteans bring many Earth animal species and plants with them, which thrive and have since been integrated into the colony planet's ecosystem. One of the evolutionary differences over the past 12,500 years is the physical size of most former Earth animals that have evolved to be *larger* on Atlantis.

The Atlanteans refer to many of the predator animals as **sha**, and differentiate them from land, sea, and sky animals. *Sha* are the dangerous animals, thought to be creations of the old darkness god. Thus, a shark is a kind of *sha*, but a *sha* might be any of a number of animals including a shark. For example, a *tif-nu-sha* is a water *sha*, which is the evolved version of an ancient Earth shark.

Other animals originally from Earth are mentioned. The crocodile evolves to become *sebeku*, the dolphin is a *delphit*, and a horse is a *sesemet*. A smaller, quick *irt* antelope evolves from a gazelle or tsessebe, while herds of the larger *yatet* antelope are reminiscent of the wildebeest. And the extremely large orange cats called *senef sedjet* may have come from tigers or jaguars. There are also many species of birds, and large insects, including the evolved scarab.

The Ancient Atlanteans bring many different food crop varieties and edible plants with them from Earth, and a few favorite ornamental plants such as the ancient **rose** and the **lotus**. Unfortunately, unlike the animals, the Earth plants do not flourish as well in the new environment with a brighter sun and different soil. Except for rare specimens in the controlled environments of greenhouses, most either die out or evolve into much different species after being crossed with or grafted onto local plants in a desperate attempt to keep them viable. A few manage to evolve or continue to be manually crosspollinated. Attempts to genetically manipulate Earth and native plants are rarely successful. In addition, there is always the issue of plant species becoming inedible, not nutritious, or even poisonous.

This is why modern Atlanteans are so excited to have original Earth plant species seeds and crops brought once again to the colony planet on the Earth Mission together with the recent Earth refugees. Atlanteans will once again be able to consume long-dead grains such as wheat, rye, barley, amaranth, rice, and other ancient favorites in their vegetarian diet! And this time, by combining their knowledge of growing plants on Atlantis with agricultural advances on Earth, they should have a much better chance of enabling these plants survival in the long term.

The Moons of Atlantis

When Gwen first arrives on her new home planet, there are *three* moons in the sky of Atlantis:

> **Amrevet**, or Love (largest, violet-grey)
> **Mar-Yan**, or The Rider (middle-sized, blue-grey)
> **Pegasus** (tiniest, silver)

The fourth moon, discovered later in the series, is the **Ghost Moon**. It is small, muted rose, tan-yellow, and blue-green.

"Average orbit" is the most accurate way to describe planetary or lunar orbits that have irregularities—closest and farthest *apsis points* that constantly vary. Such moons sometimes approach closer, and at other times move farther away from their home planet—and each other.

Generally speaking, the four moons of Atlantis have an unusual orbital system. They do not orbit along the same flat plane. Furthermore, their orbit shapes are not circular, but strongly eccentric. In other words, the moons don't revolve around Atlantis in concentric circles relatively parallel to each other. Instead, they move in wildly diverging ellipses along different rotational planes.

As a result of this oddball orbital motion, at some point all the moons make closer approaches to Atlantis—and to each other, encroaching on each other's general orbits and even passing them—before moving farther apart.

Ironically, this unique wobbly rotation is the only way that the complex *astroctadra* **alignment** becomes possible in 3D space.

However, despite their irregularities, the moons have a *general order of proximity* to Atlantis, based on their average orbital distance.

Tiny **Pegasus**, both smallest and usually closest to Atlantis, is approximately half the size of the Earth's single moon. **Mar-Yan** is the middle child, at two-thirds of the Moon's size, and usually orbits between Pegasus and Amrevet. **Amrevet** is the largest, with an orbital distance comparable to Earth's Moon (while being almost twice its size), and it also makes a closer approach to Atlantis at some points.

The Ghost Moon is larger than Pegasus but smaller than Mar-Yan in size. Its orbit is approximately twice as distant from Amrevet's *average orbit* as Amrevet's orbit is from Mar-Yan's. In other words, it's orbiting very far out there, farthest away from Atlantis.

The Moons of Atlantis, Largest to Smallest

1. Amrevet
2. Mar-Yan
3. Ghost Moon
4. Pegasus

Average Distance to Atlantis, Closest to Farthest

1. Pegasus
2. Mar-Yan
3. Amrevet
4. Ghost Moon

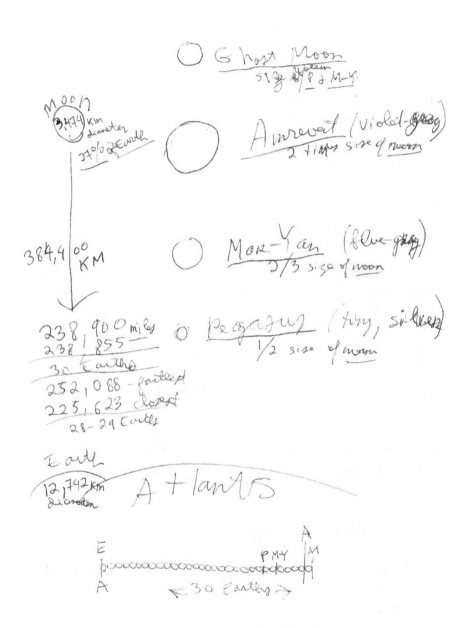

The Moons of Atlantis and Earth

CHAPTER 8 – Calendar Holidays, Dates, Seasons

The Atlantean Calendar is quite different from the Earth calendar because of the physical differences between the two planets themselves and their immediate cosmic environments.

Atlantean Day

An **Atlantean Day** has **27 hours**.

Half a day is 13 hours plus the period of "noon" and "midnight" which are each 30 minutes long. So, if you split the Atlantean day exactly in half it has 13.5 hours.

13:30 is the exact middle of the day or night.

Noon Ghost Time and **Midnight Ghost Time** begin at 13:00 and end at 13:30.

Both Noon Ghost Time and Midnight Ghost Time occupy the weird half hour between 13:00 and 00:00, for which there is no Earth equivalent.

New day begins at 00:00 (First hour).

The Atlantean equivalents of AM and PM are **"of Ra"** and **"of Khe."**
AM = of Ra
PM = of Khe

The first half of the day, the morning period before Noon Ghost Time, is ruled by Ra, while the second half of the day after Noon Ghost Time, afternoon and evening, is ruled by Khe.

The shorter intervals are expressed by antique terms.
Daydream = minute
Heartbeat = second

Atlantean Week

An **Atlantean Week** has **4 days**.

Redday, **Blueday**, **Greenday**, and **Yellowday** are standard work days. A day off, called **Ghostday**, does not occur every week but only at the end of every **two** weeks.

Days of the Week

Redday
Blueday
Greenday
Yellowday
Ghostday (the day off that comes twice a month)

Atlantean Month

An **Atlantean Month** has **6 weeks** plus only **2 days off**, so that there's a free day between each two-week period.

(4, 4, 1, 4, 4, 1, 4, 4) = 26 days

The progression order of the months is: **Amrevet, Pegasus, Mar-Yan, Ghost Moon**. This is repeated every season.

Atlantean Seasons

Atlantis has four seasons, similar to Earth, and these are the equivalents:

Earth	Atlantis
Spring	Green Season
Summer	Red Season
Autumn	Yellow Season
Winter	Blue Season

Each **Atlantean Season** has **4 months**.

The four months in order are:

1. Amrevet
2. Pegasus
3. Mar-Yan
4. Ghost Moon

They are differentiated by each seasonal designation. For example, the first month of spring (Green Season) is **Green Amrevet**. The first month of summer (Red Season) is **Red Amrevet**. The first month of fall (Yellow Season) is **Yellow Amrevet**. And the first month of winter (Blue Season) is **Blue Amrevet**.

Atlantean Year

An **Atlantean Year** has **417 days**, **16 months**, plus one last day which is **New Year Day**.

New Year's Day comes once a year, at the end/beginning between the years.

Atlantean Calendar – Months

Green Amrevet	Green Pegasus	Green Mar-Yan	Green Ghost Moon
Red Amrevet	Red Pegasus	Red Mar-Yan	Red Ghost Moon
Yellow Amrevet	Yellow Pegasus	Yellow Mar-Yan	Yellow Ghost Moon
Blue Amrevet	Blue Pegasus	Blue Mar-Yan	Blue Ghost Moon
New Year's Day			

Atlantean Calendar Year 9771

Quarter 1

Amrevet					Pegasus					Mar-Yan					Ghost Moon				
Redday	Blueday	Greenday	Yellowday	Ghostday	Redday	Blueday	Greenday	Yellowday	Ghostday	Redday	Blueday	Greenday	Yellowday	Ghostday	Redday	Blueday	Greenday	Yellowday	Ghostday
1	2	3	4		1	2	3	4		1	2	3	4		1	2	3	4	
5	6	7	8	9	5	6	7	8	9	5	6	7	8	9	5	6	7	8	9
10	11	12	13		10	11	12	13		10	11	12	13		10	11	12	13	
14	15	16	17	18	14	15	16	17	18	14	15	16	17	18	14	15	16	17	18
19	20	21	22		19	20	21	22		19	20	21	22		19	20	21	22	
23	24	25	26		23	24	25	26		23	24	25	26		23	24	25	26	

Quarter 2

Amrevet					Pegasus					Mar-Yan					Ghost Moon				
Redday	Blueday	Greenday	Yellowday	Ghostday	Redday	Blueday	Greenday	Yellowday	Ghostday	Redday	Blueday	Greenday	Yellowday	Ghostday	Redday	Blueday	Greenday	Yellowday	Ghostday
1	2	3	4		1	2	3	4		1	2	3	4		1	2	3	4	
5	6	7	8	9	5	6	7	8	9	5	6	7	8	9	5	6	7	8	9
10	11	12	13		10	11	12	13		10	11	12	13		10	11	12	13	
14	15	16	17	18	14	15	16	17	18	14	15	16	17	18	14	15	16	17	18
19	20	21	22		19	20	21	22		19	20	21	22		19	20	21	22	
23	24	25	26		23	24	25	26		23	24	25	26		23	24	25	26	

Quarter 3

Amrevet					Pegasus					Mar-Yan					Ghost Moon				
Redday	Blueday	Greenday	Yellowday	Ghostday	Redday	Blueday	Greenday	Yellowday	Ghostday	Redday	Blueday	Greenday	Yellowday	Ghostday	Redday	Blueday	Greenday	Yellowday	Ghostday
1	2	3	4		1	2	3	4		1	2	3	4		1	2	3	4	
5	6	7	8	9	5	6	7	8	9	5	6	7	8	9	5	6	7	8	9
10	11	12	13		10	11	12	13		10	11	12	13		10	11	12	13	
14	15	16	17	18	14	15	16	17	18	14	15	16	17	18	14	15	16	17	18
19	20	21	22		19	20	21	22		19	20	21	22		19	20	21	22	
23	24	25	26		23	24	25	26		23	24	25	26		23	24	25	26	

Quarter 4

Amrevet					Pegasus					Mar-Yan					Ghost Moon				
Redday	Blueday	Greenday	Yellowday	Ghostday	Redday	Blueday	Greenday	Yellowday	Ghostday	Redday	Blueday	Greenday	Yellowday	Ghostday	Redday	Blueday	Greenday	Yellowday	Ghostday
1	2	3	4		1	2	3	4		1	2	3	4		1	2	3	4	
5	6	7	8	9	5	6	7	8	9	5	6	7	8	9	5	6	7	8	9
10	11	12	13		10	11	12	13		10	11	12	13		10	11	12	13	
14	15	16	17	18	14	15	16	17	18	14	15	16	17	18	14	15	16	17	18
19	20	21	22		19	20	21	22		19	20	21	22		19	20	21	22	
23	24	25	26		23	24	25	26		23	24	25	26		23	24	25	26	

 Another good visual full-color example of an Atlantean calendar year can be found on the **Atlantean Calendar Date Converter** website: http://tag.fan/TAG-Calendar.html

Holidays:

Atlantis has many holidays, some regional, some national, and they vary from place to place. However, the following **international holidays** represent truly ancient, universal traditions, stemming from the Original Colony period and the time of Landing. They are celebrated in Imperial *Atlantida* and nearly everywhere else around the planet.

The international holidays are:

Holiday	Season	Date
Landing Day	Green Season	Green Amrevet 1 *First day of the year.*
Flower Day	Green Season	Green Mar-Yan 18
Burning Night	Red Season	Red Pegasus 22
Gold Harvest	Yellow Season	Yellow Ghost Moon 26
Light Feast	Blue Season	Blue Ghost Moon 10
New Year's Day	Comes once a year, at the end-beginning between the years, falling after *Blue Ghost Moon 26* and before *Green Amrevet 1* (which is Landing Day).	

+ As the year grows dark, **Light Feast** is celebrated in the coldest heart of Blue Season, when families gather around feast tables and light cozy bright fires to keep the cold away. Colorful lights are used to decorate everything. Light orbs, ranging from tiny to large, float in the air, and sparkling embers and fireworks bring joy in the darkness.

✦ In contrast, **Burning Night** happens in the hottest middle of Red Season when a different kind of fire is lit. Bonfires fill the dark night, filled with dancing and wild fun.

✦ **Gold Harvest** takes place during Yellow Season, a day when Atlanteans eat and remember the past, the good things and the people they love. Gifts of sweet desserts and fruit are exchanged and songs are sung.

✦ Smack in the middle of the Grail Games, there is **Flower Day** in Green Season, when Atlanteans get dressed up in garlands and everyone must wear fresh flowers or get teased. Flowers rain down on crowds in festive displays.

✦ And, of course there is **Landing Day**, to commemorate the ancient Original Colony of Old *Atlantida*, at the site of Poseidon, where stands the colossal Atlantis Grail monument of orichalcum and gold. Small ornamental grails are given out as party favors and are featured in decorations. Families have formal meals where they read passages from ancient scrolls containing historical accounts of the Early Days.

✦ The year ends on a bright note with **New Year's Day** which is celebrated all day long with family and friends around a feast table. Songs are sung and words spoken to bid farewell to the old year and welcome the new, including a special song in memory of those who were lost that year.

At the end of the day, during Midnight Ghost Time, everyone stands up and tosses a coin (or several coins) into a decorated common bowl centerpiece for good luck, and to make a bell tone ring. Embraces are exchanged, and everyone enjoys a piece of New Year's Day traditional dessert *jeleleo*, similar to *eos* pie but family sized and full of rare condiments. *Jeleleo* is a unique treat eaten only **once a year** on that day and only **during** Midnight Ghost Time (between

13:00 and 13:30 of Khe) before the final heartbeat of the day, Null Hour (considered to be the true last moment of the old year).

After the celebration is over, the bowl full of coins is left outside the door (together with any leftover *jeleleo*, which is highly uncommon) or given to charity.

Fun Random Calendar Facts

+ **Qualify** begins in March, 2047.

+ **Compete** begins in June, 2047.

+ **Win** begins in June 2048, which is 5.5 months before Asteroid Impact on Earth.

+ **Survive** begins in August, 2048 / Green Mar-Yan, 9771.

+ From the time of Gwen's arrival on Atlantis, there are approximately **3,792 hours** before the day of impact.

+ **Asteroid Impact** – November 18, 2048, 2:47 PM Eastern (Atlantis: Red Mar-Yan 17, 9771).

+ Every Atlantean Month has **702 hours**. In contrast, Earth Months are variable—February has 672 hours, but 31-day months are 744 hours long, and 30-day months have 720 hours.

Birth Dates

The following are birth dates and birthdays (not always the same thing) of some of the main characters, using both the Earth Calendar and the Atlantean Calendar.

Character	Home Planet Birth Date	Converted to Alien Calendar
Aeson	Blue Amrevet 21, 9751	September 9, 2023
George	July 24, 2029	Red Pegasus 25, 9756
Gwen	May 25, 2030	Green Amrevet 9, 9757
Gordie	February 7, 2033	Green Mar-Yan 2, 9759
Gracie	August 14, 2034	Red Amrevet 25, 9760

Fun Fact: There is an Atlantean Zodiac, with its own astrological signs, and it will be explored in detail in another volume.

Other Important Dates

✦ Ancient Atlanteans left Ancient Earth on **April 22, 10,504 BCE**. (April 22, 10,504 BCE = April 22, **12,552 YEARS AGO** from 2048!)

✦ Atlanteans spent **2 years in space** before arriving on Atlantis and establishing the first colony.

✦ **Landing Day** (on Atlantis) – **Green Amrevet 1, Year 0,** which
is be **equivalent of Earth 12,552 years** converted to Atlantean
years, plus months and days ago from *Green Ghost Moon 1, 9771,
Redday*, the day after Gwen raised the Grail and won the Games.

✦ **Time of Arrival** of Earth Mission Fleet in orbit of Atlantis:
7:24 AM Earth UTC / 11:17 of Ra, Poseidon Time

✦ **Green Amrevet 22, 9771 / June 1, 2048** – Gwen arrives on
Atlantis (end of **Compete**).

✦ November 18, 2048, 2:47 PM Eastern Time – **Asteroid Impact**.

Time Calculation

There is no 27-hour clock on Atlantis. Instead, the clock uses 13 hours twice, plus two half-hour periods for the Ghost Time.

CLOCK	
00:00:00 - 00:00:00	Null Hour *(see explanation below)*
00:00 - 01:00	1st Hour
01:00 - 02:00	2nd Hour
02:00 - 03:00	3rd Hour
03:00 - 04:00	4th Hour
04:00 - 05:00	5th Hour
05:00 - 06:00	6th Hour
06:00 - 07:00	7th Hour
07:00 - 08:00	8th Hour
08:00 - 09:00	9th Hour
09:00 - 10:00	10th Hour
10:00 - 11:00	11th Hour
11:00 - 12:00	12th Hour
12:00 - 13:00	13th Hour
13:00 - 13:30	Ghost Time *(half an hour)*

✦ Ghost Time is technically 13:00:00 – 13:30:00 twice a day.

✦ **Null Hour** (not really an "hour" but called so in the vernacular) is a **MOMENT** at **13:30:00 (or 00:00:00)** twice a day.

✦ The second Null Hour ends the day.

✦ Since Ghost Time is **appended to the end of the previous part** of the day it ends at the end of that 13-number cycle, so the 00:00 only applies to the beginning of the next one.

✦ And yes, Ghost Time is literally a "ghost" span of time attached to the final portion of the half-day period, so each 27-hour day is divided into two halves of 13.5 hours. Therefore, the **exact halfway point of the day** falls at the moment of Null Hour (00:00:00), right *after* Ghost Time ends.

Fun Fact: Time on Atlantis is measured in hours, daydreams (minutes), and heartbeats (seconds).

✦ The equivalents of **AM** and **PM** are **"of Ra"** (morning half of the day) and **"of Khe"** (evening part of the day).

✦ When talking about Ghost Time, no need to say "of Khe" or "of Ra" since Ghost Time is specified as **Noon** or **Midnight**.

So, ten minutes into Ghost Time it would be:

- "Noon Ghost Time 10" or "13:10 of Ra"
- "Midnight Ghost Time 10" or "13:10 of Khe"

✦ Ghost Time always comes at the end of the first or second part of the day period. So, **Ra** or **Khe** is assigned based on the preceding period.

CHAPTER 9 – Ages on Earth and Atlantis

A year on the colony planet Atlantis lasts 417 Atlantean days or approximately 469 Earth days. An Atlantean day is approximately 27 Earth hours. As a result, the ages of the characters mentioned in these books are *not equivalent* to the ages of humans on Earth. For example, a seven-year-old on Atlantis is nine on Earth, while a ten-year-old on Atlantis is twelve or thirteen in Earth years.

Here's a handy age conversion chart.

Atlantis age — Earth age

Atlantis age	Earth age
7	9
8	10
9	11.5
10	13
11	14
12	15.5
13	17
14	18
15	19
16	20.5
17	22
18	23
19	24.5
20	26
25	32
30	38
35	45
40	51
50	64
60	77
70	90

Furthermore, the societal norms on Atlantis have evolved differently than on Earth, with earlier maturity, education, and levels of responsibility, due to reasons and circumstances explained in **Survive**. Atlanteans begin to take on adult responsibilities, work, and perform highly skilled tasks in society very early in their lives.

Discover your **Atlantean Birthday** (and more fun facts) on the **Atlantean Calendar Date Converter** website: http://tag.fan/TAG-Calendar.html

CHAPTER 10 – Music of The Atlantis Grail

Music plays an immense part in Atlantean culture, permeating every aspect of daily life. An average person *sings* multiple *voice command sequences* every day to perform household tasks—such as calling the hovering video screen over from its place on the wall, to moving heavy objects, furniture, cooking implements, and levitating machinery. Vehicles require voice commands to drive and maneuver.

But music for pleasure and entertainment also plays an essential role in everyday existence. Atlanteans listen to music both live and recorded, and opera is revered as one of the highest arts. Notably, Atlantean opera is quite different from the version originally developed in Italy and is more like the styles of performance in the Far East and Middle East, in particular the traditional Chinese, Indian, and Persian vocalizations. But they certainly appreciate the various modern Earth performances of all the different styles.

Skilled vocalists are prized for their aesthetics and elegant technique, and also for their ability to work in the technology sector.

Earth Songs Mentioned in the Books

The following is a list of the Earth songs mentioned (by title) in the series so far.

"Feste's Song" from William Shakespeare's *A Midsummer Night's Dream*
"Bad Romance" – Lady Gaga (Gwen and Logan's breakup song)
"500 Miles" – Peter, Paul, and Mary
"Bohemian Rhapsody" – Queen
"The Habanera" – aria from the opera *Carmen* – Bizet
"Caribbean Blue" – Enya (Gwen and Aeson's song)
"Can't Help Falling in Love" – Elvis Presley
"Moondance" – Van Morrison
"Stand by Me" – Ben E. King

"Make Someone Happy" – Jimmy Durante
"The First Time Ever I Saw Your Face" – Roberta Flack
"At Last" – Etta James
"Orinoco Flow" – Enya
"La Isla Bonita" – Madonna (Manala and George's song)

In addition, although never mentioned in the series, the song "Thunderstruck" by AC/DC inspired the author while writing the final Triathlon racing scene in Stage Four of the Games.

Also, the author feels that the song "California Dreamin'" (the Sia version, released and heard by the author long after **Qualify** was already published) really invokes the Semi-Finals race through the streets of Los Angeles.

Fake Earth Bands

Two made-up bands in particular are of note.

One of the globally popular bands on Earth at the time of the Qualification period (2047) is the international sensation boy band **Ave Murakko**, and their dance hit song "Asteroid Burning Love" is requested to be played at the Yellow Zero-G Dance.

Unfortunately (or fortunately) we have only two known lines of lyrics from the song:

> Scorch me, burn me, asteroid love!
> Scorch me, burn me, crazy space m-a-a-a-n!

Then, once the Earth refugees arrive on Atlantis, an all-female girl band is formed, calling themselves the **Gebi Girls**. During the Green Zero-G Dance up in orbit at the Atlantis Station, the Gebi Girls perform a "fast and hard" song, and are mentioned by Dawn Williams:

> *"They're a recently formed band, an all-girl group of Earthies. Either four or five women in the band—I forget. They play their own instruments and sing some really good stuff, do pop covers of both old Earth and Atlantean music, and have original material too, like this song—"*

Gwen's Song to Aeson

This is an old Atlantean song, a childhood favorite of Aeson, that
Gwen sang for him during the Wedding Ceremony.

> The skies above
> Are filled with love
>
> The light of day
> Comes out to play
>
> Your holy fire
> Consumes the night
>
> Sacred desire
> Burning bright
>
> I am your spark,
> I light the way.
>
> I am your lark,
> With song I pray.

I love you to Atlantis and back!"

—Margot Lark

Eoseiara (The Wedding Song)

Eoseiara is a traditional Atlantean wedding song that is sung by the Bride and Groom both individually and in unison during the Wedding Ceremony, as they walk around the wedding chalice and light the tapers along its rim.

The word *Eoseiara* means "the dawning," "dawn-like," or "that which is of the dawn," and implies a new beginning.

The *sitahrra* mentioned in the song is an ancient traditional stringed instrument with elements reminiscent of a lute, lyre, harp, zither and even the guitar. It has a hollow wooden resonant body (usually with a round "hoop" or medallion exterior frame encircling an *astroctadra*-shaped resonance chamber—or the reverse, an *astroctadra*-shaped body with a spherical resonance chamber), a long neck and strings made of various materials including metal.

Eoseiara (The Wedding Song) – Guitar Chords
(Arrangement by Vera Nazarian)

```
E    A    A    E
Eoseiara, eoseiara,

A    A    D    A       E
Near and far, my heart longs to stay.

E    A    A    E
Eoseiara, eoseiara,

D Minor    D    A       E
Count every star, make no delay.

E    A    A    E
Eoseiara, eoseiara,
```

```
A     A    D    A    E
```
Brew in the jar, fire under clay.

```
E     A    A    E
```
Eoseiara, eoseiara,

```
D Minor   D         A        E
```
Strum the *sitahrra*, hurry, I pray.

```
E     A    A    E
```
Eoseiara, eoseiara,

```
A      A    D      A   E
```
Door is ajar, waiting all day.

```
E     A    A    E
```
Eoseiara, eoseiara,

```
D Minor      D    A        E
```
Sweetly we spar, time fades away.

```
E     A    A    E
```
Eoseiara, eoseiara,

```
A        A    D    A    E
```
I am your harbor, you are my bay.

```
E     A    A    E
```
Eoseiara, eoseiara,

```
D Minor   D    A            E
```
Over our love, nothing holds sway.

 You can hear the song ***Eoseiara*** performed by the author on YouTube: https://youtu.be/6mnCdZ4YJWI

Discover even more on the **YouTube Channel**: https://www.youtube.com/veranazarian-tag/

Amrevet-Ra – *Amrevet* Night Wedding Ritual

The following song is sung by the priests in the background and sung as a duet by Gwen and Aeson during their *Amrevet* Night. Little did they know that the song would elicit the *desire voice* in both of them—as intended!

> *Am-re-vet-Ra!*
> The serpent wakens and the fire flows
> *Am-re-vet-Ra!*
> The flower opens and the fire flows
> *Am-re-vet-Ra!*
> The serpent rises and the flower blooms
> *Am-re-vet-Ra!*

Feste's Song

"Feste's Song," also known as the Fool's Song, from *Twelfth Night* by William Shakespeare, is the song of the Four Gees, sung together in the end of **Qualify**.

> When that I was and a little tiny boy,
> With hey, ho, the wind and the rain,
> A foolish thing was but a toy,
> For the rain it raineth every day.
>
> But when I came to man's estate,
> With hey, ho, the wind and the rain,
> 'Gainst knaves and thieves men shut their gate,
> For the rain, it raineth every day.

But when I came, alas! to wive,
With hey, ho, the wind and the rain,
By swaggering could I never thrive,
For the rain, it raineth every day.

But when I came unto my beds,
With hey, ho, the wind and the rain,
With toss-pots still had drunken heads,
For the rain, it raineth every day.

A great while ago the world begun,
With hey, ho, the wind and the rain.
But that's all one, our play is done,
And we'll strive to please you every day.

—William Shakespeare, *Twelfth Night*

Music of TAG Online Resources

 We have a dedicated **Pinterest** board for TAG Music.
https://www.pinterest.com/veranazarian/music-of-the-atlantis-grail/

We also have a **YouTube Channel** that has recordings of TAG songs performed by the author, including *Eoseiara*.
https://www.youtube.com/veranazarian-tag/

CHAPTER 11 – Technology

Sound based technology is at the core of all Atlantean technology, including propulsion, space travel, medical advances, and other tools and machines.

The ability to **sing** or carry a tune allows the general population to manipulate sound-sensitive equipment made of **orichalcum**, a unique metal alloy, originally from Earth, that can be made to levitate and move by means of sound.

Voice commands consisting of different **sequences of tones** affect orichalcum at the quantum level. Over the centuries, Atlanteans have evolved and perfected the use of human voice as a unique tool to affect not only orichalcum but people.

In general, the human voice with its high level of nuance is needed for proper orichalcum manipulation, but there are some very basic tones that can be issued by instruments or recorded for automated playback to affect orichalcum for simple, low-level tasks.

Power Voices

The skills to use different **power voices** are taught to all Atlanteans from an early age.

As Nefir Mekei explains to the class of Earth teens at the Pennsylvania RQC-3, there are many different power voices.

What they hear from him first is the voice of a **Storyteller**. Certain voices are cultivated and imbued with power, to varying degrees, for specific purposes or tasks, such as **Creation, Force, Movement, Command, Desire,** or **Healing**. There are also voices of an ethically questionable nature, which are generally illegal, with very limited exceptions.

Sometimes, new or previously undocumented forms of *power voice* emerge, such as Gwen's unexpected use of the *voice of reason* or persuasion, as demonstrated in **Survive**, Chapter 8.

Due to the time it takes to master particular power voices, only the basics are taught to the Earth Candidates during the Qualification Process.

As Nefir notes, in the very short time on Earth during Qualification, there's simply not enough time for beginners to learn these complex and subtle skills that require years to cultivate. A few might discover a basic ability to do a voice or two. But everyone will be better informed about how to defend themselves from the unwanted effects of power voices.

It is indeed a form of *mind direction*, the ability to make other people **do**, or **feel**, or **think** certain things. However, true **mind control** is completely illegal in Atlantis, and misuse of voice is strictly punished and enforced.

Potentially dangerous forms of power voice may only be used with the consent of others. Indeed, standard defense techniques are taught to safeguard against it.

The strongest of the various power voices, the *compelling voice*, is used to **force others to act or think against their will**. But that is considered highly unethical, and is illegal in Atlantis culture. The only exception is for the Imperator's emergency use, and only under controlled, special circumstances.

Ability to Sing

The strong necessity in Atlantean society to have the ability to sing or **carry a tune** is illustrated powerfully by someone who is sadly *lacking* in that area—Kateb Nuletat's wife. She is the reason he enters the Games in the first place.

Yeraz Nuletat is tone-deaf and cannot sing. She can make very rudimentary musical notes, but cannot reliably replicate them. Therefore, she's unable to do even the most basic voice commands.

As a result, her limited ability to perform even the most basic common tasks (or highly skilled work) is a constant strain on her resources. In a society driven by sound technology, she's essentially disabled, and receives a negligible stipend because of her limited work options.

Kateb, a mechanical engineer, invents a medical implant device that will help her live a normal life, but in order to fully patent the device, he needs to become a Citizen. Therefore, Kateb enters the Games, risking his life to give his beloved the ability to function in a society where voice skills are a fundamental requirement.

Voice Testing Device

Remember the Atlantean sound gadget used during Preliminary Qualification at school to make the students repeat the "eeee" sounds?

This unit ranges from portable (about ten inches wide and five inches tall, such as the one at Gwen's school in Vermont during preliminary Qualification) to something large enough to take up half the desk. It looks like a strange malformed lump of perfectly seamless, silvery rock on the surface of which occasional colored lights come to life.

The person being tested must place their fingers on the surface. Then they must sing a scale, repeating exactly whatever tones the unit makes. Listen, then repeat. The indicator lights on the unit immediately respond to the person's voice and **evaluate** it.

The device checks for **pitch**, and can recognize *perfect pitch*.

It also checks for **power** and **intensity**, so that it can recognize the intensity of a high-level voice such as the Logos voice.

Red light means *off-key*, while *green* is *on-key*, bright *pale hue* means the sound is powerful, while *darker hue* means less powerful, and *white* means *Logos voice*.

Atlantean Numerals

Vera Nazarian   FEBRUARY 25, 2018

Sound Based Technology

At the heart of all is sound tech. Here are the basics.

Voice Commands

Voice commands, sung by skilled vocalists, make things happen.

Atlantean basic principles of technology involve the quantum manipulation of sound. This technology is so different from Earth tech, so original (according to Mr. Warrenson who teaches the tech class during Qualification) because it involves advanced physical interactions of wave and particle mechanics, heat and energy transfer, on a quantum level.

Atlantis technology is *based on sound.* To be precise, it is based on the interactions of various tones and frequencies and the opposing bombardment of sound waves from different directions in order to conduct, transfer and convert sound energy and in the process create physical movement and other tangible manifestations in the physical world.

It's sound, it's music—tones and notes—that make the hoverboards levitate. Sound is what makes the bulk of Atlantean tech work.

Gwen and the other Candidates are told that the basic reason why they all passed Preliminary Qualification, is that all of them can more or less *carry a tune.* Or, more specifically, replicate auditory signals correctly. This makes them prime Candidates for being able to use Atlantis technology—their computers, their engines, their mechanisms.

In a nutshell, orichalcum makes it possible to use different notes, scales, tones, and progressions of sound waves to create real usable energy.

There are **four sound divisions** within the Atlantean system.

- The Yellow Quadrant is related to sounds and musical notes classified as ***sharp***.
- The Green Quadrant represents *flat* notes.
- The Red Quadrant refers to ***major*** musical keys.
- The Blue Quadrant relates to ***minor*** musical keys.

They all have special functions and important roles and meanings in Atlantean science and physics. But all the Earth students need to know (for starters) is how to make the correct musical sounds at the appropriate times and in the right places.

Yes, there's singing involved.

Using the Yellow Quadrant as a basic approach, is a bit complicated. The Majors and Minors—Red Quadrant and Blue Quadrant—have it easy. Their sound controls are based on common musical scales.

The Yellow Quadrant and Green Quadrant's sound controls are based on *relativity*. Yellow is Sharp, while Green is Flat, so they don't really have their own reference points, as much as having to riff off the others.

To put it simply, in a musical piece, Red is the melody line, Blue is the harmony, and Yellow and Green are the counterpoints, with Yellow rising and Green falling.

Orichalcum Manipulation and Levitation

Orichalcum, the fabled metal of both Ancient Atlantis and modern, looks a little bit like **pyrite** or **fool's gold**. Under bright light it appears to catch fire and sparkle with gold flecks. But as soon as light falls away it goes back to dull grey.

Earth teens first encounter it in the hoverboards, which appear to be made of slate-grey material with gold specks in it. At the RQC classes they are given small lumps of charcoal-grey material and told that orichalcum is the basic metal alloy that Atlanteans have developed to resonate to sound. There are so many uses for it.

Despite months of testing, Earth scientists cannot understand what orichalcum really is or how it functions. The Atlanteans choose not to answer any of their questions in that regard.

The Earth scientific community, refers to the material as *orichalcum*, but considers it a placeholder name, and somewhat trite, since it is a term of mythical origins, used in ancient writings referring to an unknown, "magical" Atlantis metal. But until the Atlanteans share its atomic structure, Earth scientists have nothing else to go on. Who knows, maybe that's what the mythic orichalcum is anyway.

The weird thing is, when the Earth scientists try to analyze a sample in a lab and find out its atomic structure, they cannot properly break down this material to the atomic level. And none of the Earth science lab tests have any conclusive effect on it.

Orichalcum, the fabled metal from myth and legend, is in fact real! And it's super weird!

It is determined that it is a metal alloy. It appears to conduct heat—sometimes (which is entirely illogical). The best that scientists can conclude (an educated guess) is that part of its elemental makeup is **gold**, since gold is widely used on Atlantis for practically everything.

They have not found its melting point temperature. And everything else they *think* they know about it is messy science at best. The Atlanteans have not been particularly forthcoming with Earth about this subject nor have they shared many raw samples.

Keying Orichalcum

In order to begin working with orichalcum objects, a person needs to **key the object**.

The **keying sequence** is one of the vocalist's strongest tools in this. The vocalist needs to be precise in each note they sing, remember the correct intervals, and not hesitate.

Keying an object is the first step in being able to use it. "Keying" simply means **assuming control of an object** in order to make it perform certain functions. The first person to key an orichalcum object "claims" it—it will only work for them and no one else.

The note sequence needs to be sung in a clean, focused, precise voice.

The most **basic** keying sequence is a sustained major sequence.

C followed by short notes **E** and **G** and then **C** again, sustained. Repeat this so that it sounds like singing the components of a **C Major chord**, over and over again. Do it while you hold the orichalcum object.

At this point the lump of orichalcum begins to vibrate in the person's fingers. Once released, the piece remains in place, floating in mid-air—*levitating*.

Any other pieces of orichalcum nearby will remain **inert** if they are stored in a special **soundproof container**.

This sequence *keys* an orichalcum object to the person's unique voice and specific sound frequency or signature. The object will respond to only *that* specific voice issuing commands, until another person handles it and repeats the keying note sequence. This assures that there are no conflicting commands being issued. The Atlanteans ingeniously manipulated orichalcum so that it can exist in either *inert* or *keyed* states.

If **no one** touches an inert orichalcum object, and there are several people all singing different commands at the same time, the situation calls for ***auto-keying***. In a situation with multiple voices there is potential conflict—the orichalcum will indeed pick up and *auto-key* to the frequency of the strongest, loudest, cleanest voice. It will then respond to the first complete command sequence issued by that voice. So, the more precise and powerful the singer's notes are, the more likelihood that a person will key an object to themselves remotely.

There are two ways of **returning** orichalcum to its **inert state**.

A. Place it in a **soundproof container**. After a sufficient period of continued silence (fifteen minutes to half an hour) the auditory "charge" appears to wear out.

B. The person to whom the object is keyed must issue a "turn-off" command. Simply sing a few random notes that are ***dissonant***—notes that sound "jarring" or weird together and don't make good harmony or melody.

Motion Commands

To make an object **rise**, the vocalist sings a loud **C** note and holds it for a few seconds, then sweeps up an octave, and concludes on another C, except one **octave higher**.

As a result, any keyed object will begin to ascend.

To halt the rising motion, the vocalist sings the familiar **C-E-G** looping sequence and the object will stop moving and just levitate.

To **lower** an object or bring it back down, the vocalist sings a C note, starting in a higher octave, then sweeps down an **octave** to the lower C. The levitating object will gently float down.

And that's the basics of Atlantean object movement. The only other basic command is the **"advance forward"** command. The vocalist simply **holds** a single note. Usually it's C, or the first note of the chord chosen for the keying command sequence—that's the *tonic* note.

As already mentioned, the Red Quadrant uses Major keys and chords, so it's quite common to use C notes and Major sequences by default in general demonstrations. But it's fine to use any chord sequence, Major or Minor. The Blue Quadrant often uses D Minor. Yellow and Green commands are more complicated and advanced.

Maneuvering orichalcum objects **around obstacles** is like a game of ping-pong. It involves an *avoidance exchange* so that pieces do not collide, but instead go around each other smoothly. The vocalist makes three quick staccato notes, followed by one long one, sustained. Minor note sequences, to maneuver **below**. Major note sequences to pass **above**. Half-step up for a sharp note to go around and pass on the **right**. Half-step down for a flat note to go around and pass on the **left**.

Load Capacity of Orichalcum

The ability to hover its own weight plus carry additional weight is dependent on the **mass** of orichalcum present. For example, **one cubic inch** of pure orichalcum can support up to **twenty pounds** of weight in Earth's gravity.

It is also possible to levitate an object with a partial, small amount of orichalcum present in its makeup, including gadgets and clothing. That's one of its experimental uses. Earth scientists recognize that orichalcum, in properly measured weight amounts, strategically worn on the body can theoretically create a commercial *flying suit*.

But Atlanteans are unwilling to part with sufficient amounts of it for Earth to experiment on a large scale and actually make useful things (while still unable to properly *break down* orichalcum under lab conditions). The only known method of using it "raw" is as the building-block material in Atlantean 3D printers.

Hoverboards

The standard Atlantean **hoverboard** is a long, flat board that is **six feet** (72 inches) tall, **two inches** thick, and **twelve inches** across. It appears to be lightweight, made of a matte, non-reflective material, usually charcoal grey in color. The top and bottom do not extend straight across into a cutoff like a rectangle but instead are curved smoothly, oval and tapered off, so there are no hard edges. When inert, it is usually held upright in one hand resting the lower end against the floor.

It resembles an Earth snowboard, skateboard, or surfboard.

For the sake of beginner Earth teens, the basic Pre-Qualification hoverboards are pre-programmed to obey simple spoken English commands:

"Ready!" – levitate six inches from the floor.
"Go!" – move forward at a slow pace.
"Descend!" – come down at a very gradual slope incline.
"Level!" – taper off descent and continue moving forward.
"Stop!" – freeze and levitate in place.
"Reverse!" – do a 180° turnaround.
"Rise!" – rise in the air at a gradual slope.
"Return!" – return to original starting position six inches above the floor.

The hoverboard commands used by the teens during their first evaluation are spoken verbal sequences. But once they are Preliminary Qualified, they have to switch to singing tones.

There are no bindings to hold the rider's feet and shoes in place on the hoverboard. The rider must stand and balance their weight, and be ready to jump off at a moment's notice.

So how much weight can one hoverboard support?

No one knows how much orichalcum is in a hoverboard. However, since a hoverboard can easily support several full-grown adults and stacked boxes of heavy equipment simultaneously, there must be a significant amount.

We know that one cubic inch of orichalcum can **support 20 pounds**. We know that hoverboards measure 72 inches long, 12 inches across, and 2 inches thick.

To figure out a maximum amount of weight an Atlantean hoverboard could support on Earth, multiply 72 x 12 x 2 to reveal that there are 1,728 cubic inches per hoverboard. Multiplied by 20 pounds, that means each hoverboard can hold a maximum of **34,560 pounds** of weight!

Given that one ton equals 2,000 pounds, a hoverboard can carry just over 17 tons!

One hoverboard can carry *seventeen tons* of freight in Earth's gravity.

Granted, the assumption of Earth scientists is that hoverboards are pure orichalcum. But the specific 17-ton weight limit has not been sufficiently verified. Hoverboards could just as well be made of only thin veneer layers of orichalcum applied over other inert materials.

Aural Block

The **Aural Block** is considered an advanced command used only by the more skilled vocalist practitioners.

It's the ability to *override* and temporarily *nullify* other people's keyed orichalcum.

Strong vocalists can take an object that someone else has keyed and re-key it to **themselves**. To do this, they must first nullify the original keying, rendering the object inert, and then re-key it, usually remotely. The new vocalist sends such a strong charge that other people cannot key it back again for a long time.

This way a powerful enough vocalist can perform the Aural Block and take orichalcum objects away from other people. This enables adults to take dangerous objects away from young children, or to pass along and transfer objects to others, especially in manufacturing.

"Frying" Orichalcum

While Aural Blocks are immensely powerful standard tools in the advanced vocalist's arsenal, there is an even more powerful, but completely destructive override.

Something that can **break through** an Aural Block and in the process, **destroy** the orichalcum object being manipulated.

The command includes a very strange, intensely piercing tone that is combined with a low rumbling vibrato. The sound is rich, tangible, and *awful*.

The orichalcum object at which this command is directed will emit a brief flash and fall down, inert and dead. It now appears duller in color than normal orichalcum—the usual patina of gold flecks is missing from the charcoal grey.

It's "fried"—in other words, broken, scrambled, and its quantum atomic structure completely disrupted. It is no longer orichalcum, but something else.

"Frying" orichalcum involves a complex set of jarring notes that rearranges the quantum molecular structure of an orichalcum object to make it something else.

Logos Voice

The **Logos voice** is so much more than a power voice. At first, it appears to be a cultural phenomenon and a symbol of power, considered a genetic rarity, and attributed to only a privileged few— for centuries.

The superficial understanding is, this natural *power singing voice* is only found among the most ancient families on Atlantis. And these days, only the members of the Imperial Family still wield the ability to sing like that.

Historians recall that in the early days, thousands of years ago, they would sing to move rocks and mountains, to align things of immense weight, to move and build pyramids and erect cities.

Later, after the Ancient Atlanteans escape to the stars, the ancients on Earth come to refer to it as ***Logos anima mundi***, but soon forget the original meaning, and indeed eventually forget the voice itself. But the Logos voice is not only the **soul of the world**, it is the ancient **voice of creation**.

After it is revealed and confirmed that Gwen Lark, a common Earth girl, has the Logos voice, the Atlanteans on the Earth Mission begin to question how *she* can have the Logos voice on Earth, contrary to all their assumptions. After all, it's supposed to be practically extinct, the genetic code long gone from the Earth *homo sapiens* DNA. How is it possible?

If only there was more time (before the deadly asteroid strike) to retest samples of the population. . . .

However, as events progress, and other individuals are found to have the Logos voice, there are even more questions.

The answers come only when the ancient enemy, "They," reveal the true nature of the Logos voice, as *they* reveal the true nature of the Kassiopei bloodline.

The original humans (Kassiopei) are supposed to **share themselves** with the rest of humanity that comes after. Designated as priests by their mysterious makers, they are supposed to **serve the spirit of all the living with the Logos voice of creation**. (Instead, the Kassiopei set themselves apart, and claim the Logos voice for their own—with this and other regrettable actions precipitating the "Fall" of humanity.)

In truth, the Logos voice belongs to all, and anyone can summon the inner resources to wield it—if the **need** and the **focus** is strong enough.

This is the key to the true nature of the Logos voice. **Focused intent**, not genetics.

And yet, there is one more aspect that is to be revealed more fully—the connection of the Logos voice with its next-level power capacity to the subtle mystery of wielding universal Starlight.

The prequel series *Dawn of the Atlantis Grail* will unravel more answers!

Plural Voice

Plural Voice is a single voice command, but sung by a **vocalist chorus**.

This very advanced vocal technique is used rarely, and is very difficult to get a handle on. It involves two or more individuals singing the same command in unison, directed at the same subject.

It's not ordinary monophony. It requires great focus and precision to join multiple voices into one objective. As a tool, Plural Voice reinforces the *strength* of any voice commands to such a degree that they are practically unbreakable by anyone.

It is possible to super-lock everything with a ***Plural Voice Aural Block***.

An individual needs to be pitch-perfect and in razor-sharp *focus* in order to attempt to override the effects of Plural Voice.

Plural Logos Voice

A Logos voice is one of the few that can break a Plural Voice Aural Block and affect every object in the vicinity. It feels almost tangible as it creates the quantum-level instability necessary to take control of the orichalcum. And then it sets a new Aural Block, with all the strength and intensity of its potential.

In general, Plural Voice refers to ordinary (but highly skilled and advanced) vocalist voices. Now, imagine **several Logos voices** raised together in a chorus, filled with common intent.

Under normal circumstances, two or more Logos voices (such as Gwen and Aeson) *singing commands together*, even casually, is best to be avoided. There's just too much power and too much potential damage due to unexpected effects.

However, when it becomes necessary, a **Plural Logos Voice** chorus has the ability to do things **no one else** can.

The power and beauty of the sound they make is hard to describe. The Logos voices mix and entwine, forming a river of glorious sound that swells into a cosmic-scale *sound ocean* and fills the surrounding area with a strange, almost tangible, sonic *structure*. There is tonal intertwining happening in real time. Particle-wave-strings of energy and matter are being pulled into artful constructs.

This is why multiple Logos voices joined together in song are a **dangerous** thing.

Everything that has any trace of orichalcum content in the immediate vicinity is now connected to the Plural Logos Voice chorus on a bizarre, personal, quantum level.

It is all theirs to control—if they so choose.

The Compelling Voice

The *compelling power voice* is the only kind of *power voice* that is **restricted in use** to the reigning **Imperator** and forbidden to everyone else.

The reason for the restriction is the damaging nature of this particular power voice, and the harmful effect it has on the subject. The sole exception for the Imperator is based on the assumption that the Kassiopei are the most skilled vocalists and are the only ones able to perform this difficult task properly.

"You have no idea what you're asking, Candidate Lark. It's not rude—it's *illegal*."

Gwen wants to know why didn't Aeson simply use a *compelling voice* to just command the terrorists to stop and surrender during the hostage takeover in **Compete**.

Gennio and Anu give a good explanation.

The kind of *power voice* that *compels* others is illegal. It's really bad. No one on Atlantis is allowed to use it, except the Imperator. But the Imperator is not going to use it either, unless it's under very rare,

carefully controlled special circumstances, such as formal ritual at
Court, or during an emergency. Even the Imperial Crown Prince (who
will be Imperator one day) is not permitted by law to use it, not even
in the middle of a life-and-death fight—not until he is Imperator.

There's a good reason it's illegal to *compel*. Throughout history,
whenever the *compelling voice* was used, there were many bad
reactions, damage to the minds of the recipients, and some awful side
effects. That's why they stopped allowing it. It causes **irreversible
brain damage** in some people, and the effects in general are
unpredictable.

For one thing, it doesn't always work the way it's intended.
People's minds and brains are wired differently, so when they are
compelled, they may do *weird* things. If you compel a person to drop
their weapon, for example, one person may hesitate and fire first, *then*
drop, so it's not safe.

Not to mention it affects *everyone* in hearing range. If the
compelling voice is used during armed conflict, everyone, including
one's own military forces, would be affected by the command.

On the other hand, the Imperator uses it under **controlled
circumstances** such as during rare ceremonial ritual (to synchronize
individuals or large groups into performing perfectly timed, unified
actions), or emergency circumstances such as during times of war.
Even so, special earplugs are issued to the Imperial special forces.

Special earplugs against *compelling voice* are part
of standard combat gear. In the old days they used
to issue them to all soldiers because of random
unpredictable enemy attacks and no defense
against sonic weapons. Now, modern high-tech
sonic dampeners can easily nullify most sonic
weapons in combat, but special forces still require
the extra protection.

And the strongest reason for average individuals to never use the *compelling voice* is that the **dire responsibility** for causing someone a probable injury is best left to the one in power—the Imperator.

Quantum Stream

The Quantum Stream is the Atlantean method of **high-speed space travel**. It involves entering a special *quantum flux state* which exists outside of normal space-time in relation to our physical universe. In a sense it means becoming a "quantum ghost" as you flow and stream through the universe at unimaginable speeds unrelated to the speed of light, only to the fabric of the universe itself.

This is how Earth Mission Commander Manakteon Resoi describes their journey to the Earth refugees:

> *"We start this journey and leave Earth's orbit tomorrow, at exactly 8:00 AM, Earth Universal Time Coordinated, accelerating gradually. In about a week we will be outside your solar system. And then we will continue accelerating for six months, reaching incredible speeds within a special physical flux-state called a Quantum Stream, at which point we will Jump, crossing an immense light years distance in a blink, and emerge far in the Constellation of Pegasus. There we will decelerate for another six months, then emerge out of the Quantum Stream and arrive in our new solar system on Atlantis."*

Once the Fleet enters the Quantum Stream, it is important that the ships align together in a balanced formation and not pass a certain boundary of their "bubble," else they accidentally **Breach** and end up literally anywhere in the universe (between here and there) with no real means of getting back in.

Earth Cadets are taught safety rules and the **Quantum Stream Breach Emergency Protocol** which includes the **QSBEP-1 Emergency Instructions** on how to return back inside the Stream. The instructions are assumed to be worthless, and mostly for morale. See *CHAPTER 13 – Earth Mission: Ark-Ship Layout, Shuttles* for the detailed emergency instructions.

While inside the Stream, trained pilots can fly from ship to ship in the formation, and can even rendezvous with the Stream from the outside if they are given exact coordinates and frequency, and the whole thing is perfectly timed.

Meanwhile, the **QS races** are held to teach beginner Earth Cadets how to maneuver. Flying in the same direction as the Fleet is heading is called *streaming*. Flying in the opposite direction, against the Quantum Stream is called *ripping*.

It is of note that the Quantum Stream can be Stationary, a very difficult procedure done by the Imperator, such as during the Rim Maintenance Missions to reinforce the Great Quantum Shield at Ae-Leiterra.

The Imperator places the entire Fleet array into a **Stationary Quantum Stream**. It's a very different kind of quantum phase state from the ordinary Quantum Stream (the kind where it's necessary to *accelerate* to enter it, and which is used to travel cosmic distances).

In contrast, the Stationary Quantum Stream needs no specific velocity, can be achieved from a fixed, or slowly drifting position, and is extremely difficult and dangerous to implement, requiring perfect precision. Only a Logos voice can be used to shape it, so the task falls to the Imperator.

The ships, phase-locked in the safety of the Stationary Quantum Stream, may approach and traverse the Rim, flying as deep as necessary. They can approach the black hole's reality horizon and even cross it safely, and enter inside. No time dilation, no radiation or other matter corruption is experienced.

That's why Atlanteans call it the reality horizon. It poses danger only when occupying this present space-time reality. Once inside any kind of Quantum Stream, the occupants are in a different reality, so they may pass safely.

Weather Control

One of the first things that Earth refugees discover once they land on Atlantis (after they experience the tedious higher gravity), is the fact that Atlantis has excellent **weather control technology**.

It seems to Gwen that the weather is always the same in Poseidon—not a cloud in the sky, and a moderate, pleasant climate.

Green Season is known for its mildness and stability. Red Season is just starting, so prepare for heat and winds.

Such rigid weather control applies mostly to the larger urban centers. There is regional weather variation, and seasonal. But to counteract the most drastic fluctuations, there's urban weather monitoring and control over the largest cities such as Poseidon.

Occasionally things break down, such as New Deshret's weather tech going haywire for some time. And then, once the Ghost Moon is reinstated, disrupting the orbital system balance and increasing the gravitational effect on the tides, all kinds of wild weather fluctuations and natural disasters begin happening on Atlantis—until they figure out how to realign and balance their weather.

Ghost Moon

As soon as the Ghost Moon "arrives," all chaos ensues on the surface of Atlantis. The moon is exerting gravitational influence on the whole local planetary system, and Atlantean weather control systems must be reprogrammed with the new parameters to compensate.

When Gwen and Oalla return from their Mar-Yan mission, they're in for a wild ride (**Survive**, Chapter 79).

There is atmospheric turbulence and *more*.

Reports indicate atmospheric gravity waves and multiple major tidal events on the surface.

Catastrophic tidal wave activity grows at the oceanic belt. Atmospheric gravity waves cause air displacement, storms, and hurricanes. Huge tidal waves form because of the new moon's gravitational pull.

In some locations, malfunctioning weather tech adds to the problems. The weather control agencies work desperately on reprogramming weather control systems to account for the gravitational effects of the new moon and regain control over the situation.

After things finally settle down, the Ghost Moon is accepted as the new normal and given a proper name.

Now, **Arlenari** (as she is called) takes her permanent place in the Atlantean star-filled night skies along with Pegasus, Mar-Yan, and Amrevet—that is, as *permanent* as relative things can be in the constantly moving, wondrous universe. And the weather control algorithm works again, this time with *four* gravitational tide-causing planetary bodies in the mix.

How did the Ghost Moon come to be in an alternate quantum state in the first place? The story is told in the prequel series ***Dawn of the Atlantis Grail***.

Weather Funnel

During Stage Two of the Games, Gwen and the other Contenders experience the effects of a **weather funnel**.

Out of nowhere, it seems, a weird cloud mass appears over the pyramid. Directly overhead, a dark circular spot takes shape. Gwen thinks of it as a "whirlpool," because it's not a tornado—the circling spiral motion is incredibly slow moving, like a circling drain in slow motion.

Chihar and Kokayi explain that it's an artificial weather funnel.

On Atlantis, weather funnels are generated on demand. Anyone can order one for their region, if they have sufficient funds to pay for it.

The kind of precipitation the customer gets is completely up to them. The weather techs control the weather funnel programming, and will serve up whatever they need.

In case of this particular weather funnel, it dispenses a crashing torrent of rain on the pyramid.

Normally the water that comes from weather funnels is neutral, intended to water crops, and is biologically safe for animal consumption.

Starlight

Technically, *Starlight* is not Atlantean technology, but the technology of the universe. It is first referenced by Erita Qwas in **Survive**, Chapter 36, together with the mention of **Arleana, Starlight Sorceress**, then in Arlenari's diary in Chapter 82.

The actual technique, and the fine, elusive nature of *Starlight* as a means of connecting across impossible distances and traversing the universe via **entanglement** is introduced in Chapter 100.

It is also explored in depth in the prequel series, *Dawn of the Atlantis Grail*.

CHAPTER 12 – The Games of the Atlantis Grail

The Games of the Atlantis Grail are at the heart of the story. They are as ancient as the time of colonization, thousands of years ago. In many ways, they inspire the brutal ethos of the modern Qualification challenges in 2047.

But here's a little secret just for you—the original ruthless challenge of winning a place on the Ancient Atlantean ark-ships to escape that first asteroid threat (an ancient version of Qualification!) influences the emergence of the Games as they later evolve on the colony planet Atlantis.

So, which came first, the chicken or the egg? Qualification or the Games? Find out as you read **Eos**, book one of the prequel series *Dawn of the Atlantis Grail* where this notion is fully explored.

Origin of the Games

We finally find out how the Games come about in **Survive** (Chapter 82), in Arlenari's diary.

Soon after Landing, the Long Sickness begins. The multiple Quantum Jumps cause the Sickness which only affects the grown adults, the old, and the very young—those with lower or diminished hormonal levels. All the adults are incapacitated, physically and mentally. They begin dying from degenerative disease. Ancient Atlantean high-tech medicine is unable to find a cure.

Only the teenagers with their hormones at the strongest levels remain healthy. (So do the Kassiopei Family and the Heru Family.)

With so many people in the colony incapacitated, the workforce is diminished. Teenagers are given adult responsibilities and put to work. *Aptitude tests* are given to everyone to ensure they are able-bodied and responsible enough to perform adult work.

Career placement is determined based on abilities, talents, and hidden strengths.

The tests look at ten labor categories:

- Warrior
- Physical Laborer
- Technician
- Scientist
- Animal Handler
- Entertainer
- Artist
- Inventor
- Merchant
- Vocalist

The tests are held seasonally. With time, they evolve, and their main objectives are so cleverly disguised that the general population begins to think of them as *games*.

The Games of the Atlantis Grail are born, their original purpose forgotten over the centuries. What starts out as career placement and aptitude tests for basic jobs turns into cruel contests for survival of the fittest, with the ultimate social rank of Citizenship as the prize.

But there is one more reason why the Games persist over time— the Kassiopei Imperators need a ceremonial reason to issue grand sequences of Voice commands in public, on site, in the Atlantis Grail Stadium.

Modern Games

The Games are Forever!

Or at least it seems that way when we first hear about them.

In the Atlantean Calendar Year 9771, when Gwen arrives on Atlantis and is forced to enter the Games by her Imperial Father-in-Law, the modern-day **Ten Categories** of Contenders are:

- Warrior (Red)
- Athlete (evolved from Physical Laborer) (Red)
- Technician (Blue)
- Scientist (Blue)
- Animal Handler (Green)
- Entertainer (Green)
- Inventor (Yellow)
- Artist (Yellow)
- Entrepreneur (evolved from Merchant) (White)
- Vocalist (White)

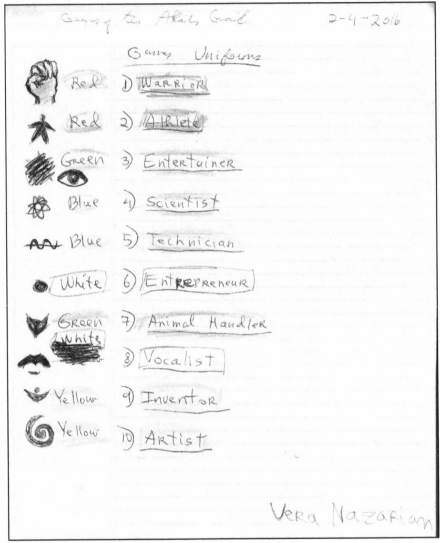

The Ten Categories and Contender Uniform Logos

    The general population of Imperial *Atlantida*—the oldest nation on the planet and the only one still continuing the tradition of the ancient "tests" in the form of the Games—is strongly hierarchical and class-based. Over time, the three major divisions of society into *nobility*, *citizens*, and *commoners*, produce insurmountable differences in lifestyle aspirations, achievements, and possible choices for individuals.

In order to break out of their static social castes and achieve their heart's desire and true life goals, an individual has to take an extreme risk and put their life on the line.

Entering the Games as a **Contender** and surviving the **Four Stages** of competition is the only sure way of getting their extreme, desperate needs met.

The **Champion** in each of the **Ten Categories** can count on the impossible—high tech medical care, highest education, land, riches, opportunities, rank and privilege. "All their wishes granted" is not a far cry from reality, as long as it's within the realm of possibility.

In addition, as a full Citizen, a person has the right to vote and make changes to the society itself and its laws, to hold high political office, enter high society, and be eligible for other positions of the highest rank in all areas of life.

But in order to become a Champion, each Contender has to be willing to **die**. Thousands of people begin in Stage One, and Ten Champions emerge at the end of Stage Four, with an additional handful of tie-breaker honorable survivors. The average odds of winning vary each year, depending on the number of entrants, but they are at least one in a thousand.

"Tell me what infernal idiot ancestor of your people was responsible for this hell experience I'm having today? Why am I going to be swimming with sharks instead of dolphins?"

—Brie Walton

As a result, the people who enter the annual Games are truly desperate. Some of them are looking for miraculous saves and cures, for resolutions to legal issues and Imperial pardons for crimes committed, and for a way out of poverty. Some of them enter because they are proud of their talents and abilities and want to achieve even more. A few of them are just nuts.

Each crop of preliminary applicants in the Pre-Games Trials inevitably has its share of celebrities—actors, orators, athletes and sports stars, courtesans, politicians, musical performers—as well as martial artists, members of the military, scientists, skilled technicians, and little-known entertainers such as street musicians, acrobats, magicians, and dancers. They easily fall into the designated Categories.

However, ordinary desperate people must also choose a Category when entering the Games. For those unknowns, without any significant talents or achievements, the two White Categories are usually the best fit—Entrepreneur and Vocalist. They serve as catch-all categories for the non-specialists.

The other more prestigious eight Categories are carefully chosen to align with the Four Cornerstone values of the Four Quadrants which evolve from the basic division of labor on the Ancient Atlantean ark-ships. Learn more about the origin of the Color Quadrants in the prequel series, ***Dawn of the Atlantis Grail***.

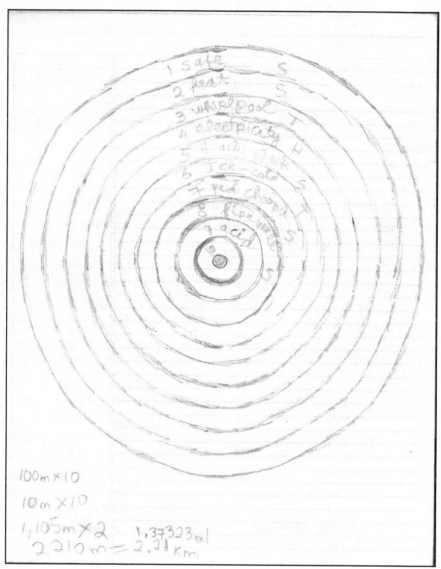

Concentric Circles of the Game Zone of Stage Three

The Rules

The specifics of Games trials and tasks are changed every year, but there are always Four Stages of competition, with the arena—called the **Game Zone**—of each stage held in a different location.

After a day of grand spectacle and the **Commencement Ceremony**, Contenders spend the night isolated in individual cells, with their equipment and weapons bags and a **Uniform** displaying the **Color** and **Logo** of their **Category**. In the morning the cells open, releasing them into the first Game Zone and they may not leave it until the end of the specific time period allocated, on pain of Disqualification.

Each Stage lasts a **week** (four days) and presents the Contenders with tests in the form of **Challenges** and **Ordeals** of varying difficulty—different ones every year—and they have to either complete and pass all the elementary tasks during each Stage, or survive long enough for the Stage to end. As Contenders participate in the Games, they earn **Atlantis Grail Points**, or **AG Points**, for everything they do and how well they do it. The number of AG Points at the end of the Games determines the winning order of **Champions**.

> **Stage One, or Red Stage** – inspired by the values of the Red Cornerstone (Passion, Aggression, Anger, Force), serves as the first outlet for everyone's violent energy. It's a test of fighting skills and physical abilities, with the most gore and bloody carnage, always held in the grand arena of the Atlantis Grail Stadium. Most Contenders are eliminated in this opening round. *Stage Winner Prize: Red Grail.* After completing the Stage, Contenders are released to spend the night outside the Games (and receive medical attention), then must return to the next designated location in the morning.
>
> **Stage Two, or Blue Stage** – inspired by the values of the Blue Cornerstone (Leadership, Control, Reason, Analysis), challenges intellectual reasoning and thinking skills. It requires complex problem solving, presents difficult mind games, and is held at an

undisclosed site announced only on the night before. *Stage Winner Prize: Blue Grail.* After completing the Stage, Contenders get the night, plus a full day off to rest outside the Games. This day serves as the halfway point in the games and always falls on the Flower Day holiday. Contenders must return to the next designated location on the morning after Flower Day.

Stage Three, or Green Stage – inspired by the values of the Green Cornerstone (Endurance, Patience, Resistance, Strength), challenges the will and determination. It is usually known as the "ordeals stage," and is held at an undisclosed site announced only on the night before. *Stage Winner Prize: Green Grail.* After completing the Stage, Contenders are released to spend the night outside the Games, then must return to the final designated location in the morning.

Stage Four, or Yellow Stage – inspired by the values of the Yellow Cornerstone (Creativity, Originality, Curiosity, Inspiration), offers the most unpredictable set of challenges, and is held at an undisclosed site announced only on the night before. *Stage Winner Prize: Yellow Grail.* This final stage is known for its weird surprises. The remaining living Contenders at the end of Stage Four are returned to the Atlantis Grail Stadium in Poseidon for the final events and Closing Ceremony.

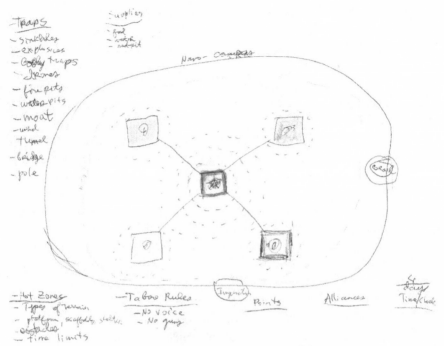

Stage One Game Zone – *Stadion* **Arena of the Games**

To win or to successfully complete (and survive) each Stage, each Contender must aim to complete a specific assigned **Task** and earn, steal, or obtain by any means the **Color Grail** of that stage. Multiple categories of points are assigned for all behavior, and additional points are earned by completing the Tasks. Points are also earned by *rendering the opponent unable to compete*—killing or disabling other Contenders—all their points are automatically assigned to the person who kills them. There are also points given for style, cleverness, and other interesting methods displayed by Contenders.

Tasks can be Ordeals or Challenges, and often *both*. Ordeals are situations that must be *endured*, while Challenges require Contenders to actively *accomplish* something.

Contenders who die or are badly injured and unable to continue, at any point in any of the Stages, are removed from the Games by the

Games staff. They are automatically Disqualified. Contenders also have the choice to Self-Disqualify.

If *everyone* in any given Category is eliminated at any point in the Games, alternate entrants are brought in from the large pool of qualified people who did not make the final cut in the Pre-Games Trials.

To increase difficulty, each Stage offers timed periods of "safety" and "danger" plus random "safe zones" (formal **Safe Bases**, or simply areas of little to no action) and "hot zones" scattered throughout the Game Zone. It may also assign various random handicaps in the form of **Taboo Rules**. When such instructions are given at any point in the Stage, Contenders are forbidden from certain actions, and if they break a Taboo Rule, they are Disqualified.

Water and food **rations** are served to the Contenders several times a day, and getting to those rations is also worth points.

Every Game Zone has some areas designated as Safe Bases where Contenders can lock themselves in and find a few extras supplies, or hide out and wait in secret. Safe Bases also have small view screens for keeping track of the competition. Finding and appropriating a Safe Base is fortunate and can grant moments or hours of badly needed rest and respite to the individual or informal team of Contenders working together.

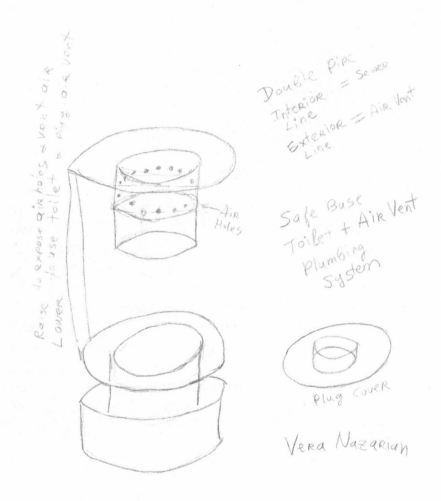

Double Pipe
Interior Line = Sewer
Exterior Line = Air Vent

Safe Base Toilet + Air Vent Plumbing System

← Air Holes

Raise to expose airholes & vent x air or pipe or vent
Lower to use toilet

Plug Cover

Vera Nazarian

Safe Base Toilet and Air Vent Schematic

As the Games progress, most Contenders find it advantageous to work with others in teams, usually consisting of people of different Categories cooperating under temporary truce, to better their chances of survival. It is almost unheard of to have **Category Rivals** on the same team. For example, two Athletes would be direct rivals for the same Champion spot. The end goal of each is to eliminate all other Athletes to win—so they could never trust the other even for a moment. This applies to every Category. But people from different

Categories do not necessarily have to kill other Category Contenders, since they are not competing for the same spot. Therefore, they can be "friends," at least for the time being.

"Who are these clowns?"

—Brie Walton

Everything comes down to AG Points. Points are constantly added or subtracted, lost upon death and inherited by the one who bested the deceased, and the running tally results are displayed live on giant scoreboards. The audience uses these numbers to make gambling bets (see *The Audience* section below).

Contenders who survive each Stage to the last moment (including the lucky Contender who has in their possession the Grail of that Stage) get to advance to the next Stage. After a night of rest (and urgent medical care), the surviving Contenders are taken to the next Game Zone where they receive a new set of instructions, and must complete new Tasks, grab another Grail, and so on. At the end of Stage Four, the remaining Contenders in each Category (apparent winners with the highest scores and a few surviving runners-up, sometimes requiring a tiebreaker during the Final Ceremony) are airlifted back to the Atlantis Grail Stadium for the final Ceremony on the last day of Green Mar-Yan, when by tradition the Games have to end.

"Yeah, whatever. As I said, Fuzzy Bottom."

—Brie Walton

There, any tie-breaker events are held, the honorable losers sent away, while the remaining Top Ten are crowned Champions.

Under normal circumstances, they are each handed out the small Grails of Champions (in addition to the Four Stage-specific Grails to their respective winners), awarded the monetary prize (usually millions of *iretar* from the Champion money pot that is evenly divided among the Ten), and administered the Oath of Citizenship by the Imperator.

In conclusion they are interviewed by the media, and are expected to attend many media events in the days to come. As Champions they are now permanent celebrities, and with that come certain responsibilities and obligations of media appearances.

Finally, within a week after the end of the Games, the Champions have to formally submit a list of their Wishes via online Champion request form to the Games Staff so that their Wish Fulfillment process can begin.

The Audience

The **Games Audience** is a vastly important part of the Games. Every moment of the Games is recorded on video, and in many cases on audio, from nearly infinite angles, utilizing **nano-cameras** (tiny, nearly invisible cameras that are released in clouds like snowflakes and can be sent anywhere) and other cameras and recording technology, so that everything is live-streamed on multiple channels. Once inside the Game Zone, Contenders have no privacy and can assume that every moment they are being stream-watched or recorded by someone.

There are potentially hundreds of aspects and feeds dedicated to every Contender, Audience members can choose to follow their favorites on small personal feeds on their personal devices, watch the gameboards and large mega-screens in the arenas, or watch in real time the live action happening directly before their eyes.

"I am speechless, even as I continue to speak..."

—Games Media Commentator

There are network shows dedicated to Games Coverage, with the two major ones (and ratings rivals) being *Grail Games Daily* hosted by Tiago Guu, and *Winning the Grail* hosted by Buhaat Hippeis, celebrity hosts and experts on the Games. The Games action is also narrated and analyzed live by professional commentators on site, who broadcast their running commentary to the venue audience and beyond.

Audience members can buy all-pass tickets to the entire Games or individual Stages (four days) or single events (such as the Opening Ceremonies) directly. They can also simply watch from home—and almost the entire population of the country does just that.

Grail Games Rage, or GGR is a know phenomenon where fans go into frenzies over the results, or betting. During the month of Green Mar-Yan in Green Season when the Games are held, many people take time off work, and many ticket holders stay up all day and night in their seats, to watch the night action (and place live bets) at the arena venue, with the help of the illegal street drug **AG Runner** (which takes away the need for sleep but wears down the body eventually, causing major mental problems, and is addictive).

Gambling on every aspect of the Games is a huge and vital part of the economy. People make and lose fortunes on live bets. And they gamble over everything—Contenders and their rank standings at any given moment, teams, various points, specific actions, results, outcomes, confrontations, deaths, skill displays—so there are millions of ways to gamble.

The Games are so deeply imbedded in the *economy* that it's truly difficult to enact any changes to the brutality or the ancient rules, even though some lawmakers make the occasional attempt. In fact, "many attempts to get rid of the Games have been made over the centuries.

The IEC is either deadlocked or votes against it, and the Imperator of the time never chooses to cast the deciding vote," Aeson explains in **Win**, Chapter 16, adding that the cruelty of the Games is "archaic, inhuman, and should have been abolished centuries ago. And yet, due to special financial interests and powerful lobbies, it persists."

So then, how can one change something that's so ingrained that it seems to be *forever*? Gwen and Aeson have what it takes to make the change.

The answer can be gleaned in **The Book of Everything**, book five of the original series.

Year 9771 Games Facts and Stats

Below are some specific facts and stats for the **Games of the Year 9771**, when Gwen was a Contender.

Games Schedule:

- **Green Mar-Yan 9** – Games Commencement Day (Contender Parade, Ceremonies).

- **Green Mar-Yan 10** – Stage One begins (day one).

- **Green Mar-Yan 13** – Stage One ends (day four).

- **Green Mar-Yan 14** – Stage Two begins (day one).

- **Green Mar-Yan 17** – Stage Two ends (day four).

- **Green Mar-Yan 18** – Flower Day, one-day holiday break from the Games.

- **Green Mar-Yan 19** – Stage Three begins (day one).

- **Green Mar-Yan 22** – Stage Three ends (day four).

- **Green Mar-Yan 26** – Stage Four ends (day four), Gwen wins the Yellow Grail, but Games Final Ceremony is disrupted by Gwen raising the Atlantis Grail Monument and wrecking the *Stadion* arena. Games are paused due to "seismic disturbance," to be concluded at a later date.

- **Green Ghost Moon 2** – Games tiebreaker events held, Champions announced, and Final Ceremony is formally concluded, ending the Games.

Contender Rules of Conduct

- You may not fight, sabotage, harm, or undermine any of the Contenders outside the Game Zone.

- You may not touch, steal, or cause damage to the equipment, weapons, bags or other Contender property outside the Game Zone.

- Intimidation, blackmail, and other dishonest methods of influence are forbidden outside the Game Zone, and verbal contact is limited except for designated circumstances.

- Weapons may not be openly carried outside the Game Zone, and must be kept in closed bags.

- You will respect your fellow Contenders and their right to privacy until the competition begins.

- You will faithfully follow the Instructions and Taboo Rules of each Stage.

- You will respect the final decisions of the Judges in regard to the awarding of AG points and disqualification.

- If you sustain a mortal injury, your designated representatives may request to have your body and your property extracted from the Game Zone before the completion of a Stage.

- You're responsible for your own property, including all your custom weapons and personal equipment bags, which must be kept with you at all times. If anyone comes in contact with your property, assume it has been compromised.

- The Games are Forever!

Final AG Points and Rank of the Ten Champions

1. **Kokayi Jeet**, Entertainer – 60,479 points
2. **Hedj Kukkait**, Warrior – 46,291 points
3. **Kateb Nuletat**, Inventor – 6,137 points
4. **Leetana Chipuo**, Animal Handler – 5,804 points
5. **Rurim Kiv**, Artist – 4,107 points
6. **Gwenevere Lark**, Vocalist – 3,972 points
7. **Gabriella Walton**, Entrepreneur – 3,821 points
8. **Mineb Inei**, Technician – 3,605 points
9. **Ukou Dwetat**, Athlete – 3,428 points
10. **Rea Bunit**, Scientist – 3,394 points

Winners of The Four Grails:

✦ *Red Grail of Stage One* – **forfeiture**, due to loss of life of Athlete **Deneb Gratu** (who fell to his death from his *pegasus*), with no clear succession or inheritance of points. The Grail is awarded to the **People** and is on display in the Imperial Poseidon Museum.

✦ *Blue Grail of Stage Two* – held by Artist Champion **Rurim Kiv**.

✦ *Green Grail of Stage Three* – originally held by Entertainer **Tiamat "Thalassa" Irtiu**, inherited by Entertainer Champion **Kokayi Jeet**.

✦ *Yellow Grail of Stage Four* – held by Vocalist Champion **Gwenevere Lark**.

Original Logo of the Atlantis Grail

CHAPTER 13 – Earth Mission: Ark-Ship Layout, Shuttles

The Earth Mission is a complex, many year-long joint mission carried out between Imperial *Atlantida* and the other nations of Atlantis. It is conceived by the Imperator Romhutat Kassiopei, in response to a terrifying revelation given to him by his own father during the last moments of his life at the Rim of Ae-Leiterra.

The true underlying reason for the mission and Romhutat's motivation are explained in **Survive** (Chapter 84).

In a nutshell, it's all about the Great Quantum Shield.

For centuries, the Great Quantum Shield holds together *everything*—the dimensional rift back on Earth, the ancient wormhole passageway at Ae-Leiterra, the various resonating components of the ark-ship, and the Ghost Moon itself. Everything is safely isolated, contained, and neutralized. All the dangerous, volatile pieces of the ancient past locked away into their own quantum realities (without being destroyed, because *their destruction itself* would bring the ancient enemy upon them).

And then, the Shield *fails*—several years ago, during a Rim maintenance mission. Romhutat's Imperial Father, Etamharat Kassiopei, dies trying to contain it and the resulting cascade reaction. His last communication to his son (relayed from his shuttle just before it succumbs to the forces of the black hole)—is a terrible revelation. The words of his message are etched permanently into Romhutat's mind.

> *"The pegasei keep coming in greater numbers— and the alien enemy will follow, to end our species. Without a Shield to protect us, you must do everything in your power to close the rift. Return to Earth, do it on site. If you find a modern human population on Earth, bring them to Atlantis. It will change our genetic pool, disguise it sufficiently to throw off the enemy's means of detection of us.*

Modern Earth DNA infused into our own will shield us now. The enemy will conclude that we are no longer the same ancient rebels who disobeyed. After all, if they spared humanity on Earth up to this day, permitted them to go on living, it is because they thought humanity had changed—evolved into something worthy of existence."

With these words, Etamharat Kassiopei dies. And the new Imperator Romhutat is determined to set the plan in action.

But he has to disguise his true mission into a grand humanitarian rescue mission to save a portion of Earth humans from yet another asteroid apocalypse, and to bring them in an armada of Fleet ships across the universe to Atlantis.

The Atlantean public is informed that their ancient extraterrestrial adversaries recently deployed an asteroid in order to finish what was started ten thousand Atlantean years ago. The Fleet is being sent to Earth on a humanitarian mission to rescue as many as possible.

Aeson originally tells Gwen that they brought the Earth teens here for more than one reason. The Atlanteans felt obligated to rescue the Earth humans, but they also needed all ten million of Earth refugees to rescue Atlantis in turn.

Officially, the Fleet needs more Cadets, more strong young *soldiers* to fight on behalf of Atlantis. This argument is used to convince the Imperial Executive Council and the governments of other Atlantean nations to agree to such great expenditures and allocation of resources necessary to bring ten million Earth refugees here.

However, much more is at stake. Imperial *Atlantida* and the other nations are stagnant. They could use more soldiers, but what they really need are scientists, artists, thinkers, and creatives with strong new ideas to imbue their civilization with fresh life and perspective. They need Gwen and others like her.

Earth refugees are not merely expendable. They are here to rescue Atlantis as a *sentient species*—to make them *better*, to give *hope*, to teach them to think in new ways, so that together they can defeat the ancient alien adversary. After thousands of years, both Earth *and* Atlantis are more advanced, stronger, and better capable of resisting and fighting back. With the integration of Earth refugees, they all stand a chance.

The Earth Mission is a true international endeavor. The government of Imperial *Atlantida* and the governments of other major nations pitch in their resources toward the rescue mission, in exchange for taking in Earth refugees.

Aeson understands how bittersweet is their rescue of Earth. But what motivates him is the knowledge that together, both populations united, they might somehow *survive*.

Meanwhile, the Atlanteans make contact and *inform* the Earth governments and the United Nations. Earth Union's highest officers are informed to some degree. Earth authorities consult via the Atlantis Central Agency with the Imperator and the IEC, and decide *not* to share with the Earth general population the harsh reality of the rescue. And Atlanteans honor their decision.

Do Earth authorities somehow already *know* about the alien threat, even before the information is shared with them? Earth seems to be in complete ignorance of any alien contact, but the IEC council members suspect there's a complicated game going on, and that Earth governments have not been completely honest with them.

Some IEC members are convinced that Earth authorities made *earlier contact* with the aliens, angered them in a similar way as the Ancient Atlanteans (which resulted in the current asteroid being deployed) and unwittingly gave the enemy enough incidental clues and information via access to Earth's historical records—which allowed the aliens to deduce the colony planet's present location, leading them here. This is pure speculation.

Thanks to the EU operatives such as Logan Sangre opening up and talking, corruption is revealed at the highest levels (going all the way up to the United States President). Special secret deals are made with the Imperator, and promises exchanged—promises he never intends to keep.

Aeson also tells Gwen about Nefir Mekei's role in all this. Nefir Mekei is an agent of the Imperator and always has been. It's a fact known and accepted by all since he was assigned as the primary Earth liaison on the Imperator's behalf.

Then Gwen and Aeson go the see the Imperator who admits that he designed the Earth Mission, every detail and component, and carefully guided all the pieces and all the players for these past several years.

The asteroid needs to strike at certain coordinates in the Atlantic Ocean, in the location of the original Atlantis continent, where it will detonate a high-level quantum energy charge.

The precisely calculated **detonation** will **close and repair** the ancient *dimensional rift* which brought the alien enemy to Earth so many eons ago. It will end their struggle once and for all.

Central Access Hub and Elevator Platform Shaft inside the Vimana

The Great Pyramid of Giza

The Great Pyramid plays an important part in the Earth Mission, because the Imperator suspects it contains ancient symbols that might shed some light on the ancient enemy.

This might seem strange since, according to official Earth historians and archeological experts, the pyramid was **built later** than Ancient Atlantis, and the Atlanteans were already long gone. Here's where the standard interpretation of the true age of the pyramid is indirectly questioned. There is also the notion that survivors of the asteroid apocalypse (or maybe their descendants) were somehow involved in its making—and symbol encoding.

Meanwhile, Atlanteans encounter **mysterious, unfamiliar symbols** in one chamber of the buried ancient ark-ship Vimana. And then, during the Earth Mission, as they are in the process of transporting the stones of the disassembled pyramid (according to the Imperator's strict instructions), these same symbols are accidentally discovered.

Because of those symbols, the Imperator specifically instructs that the pyramid is to be **included in the Games as a challenge.** They still don't know the symbols' greater meaning. Atlantean experts manage to unravel a meaningful correlation between a few of them (basic relationships between some of the shapes, no actual translation). And so, a Games puzzle is constructed, with the hope that the Contenders might figure something out in the process of solving the basic puzzle as a Game Stage Challenge.

Originally, the Great Pyramid is considered too big of a bother to bring—nothing but heavy, crudely hewn, ancient stones, with little artistic value except for sentimental historical reasons and its designation as one of the Seven Wonders of the Ancient World. The Imperial Executive Council is dead set against it, and they are officially in charge of allocating the Earth Mission resources.

But the Imperator suddenly *has his reasons*. Therefore, he makes an offer to Pharikon Heru. New Deshret would handle all the interstellar transportation expenditures of the pyramid, and they will get to keep it.

The Imperator desperately wants to have that first *look* at the pyramid before giving it up to New Deshret. So, he barters for its one-time inclusion in the Games in exchange for *Atlantida* giving up claims to Dante Gabriel Rosetti and most of the Pre-Raphaelites—which go to New Deshret also.

Once the Games are concluded, the Pyramid is transported to New Deshret where it now stands in its new permanent location near the city of Heruvar.

Fun Fact: The Statue of Liberty went to Ubasti. They were eager to claim it. The Symbol of Democracy holds a great deal more power in that nation than anywhere else on Atlantis.

Advance Scout Earth Mission: Elikara

In one of the most tragic events, in the early, preliminary stages of the Earth Mission, young **Elikara Vekahat**, fresh out of Fleet Cadet School, and her father **Qeth Vekahat**, both die under mysterious unspecified circumstances.

Her cousin Xelio is devastated, and so is Aeson—who has strong feelings for her. Aeson goes to confront his Imperial Father and learn the truth about the incident.

Unfortunately, Romhutat refuses to give any specifics, admitting only that it was during a **special tactical mission**.

Much earlier, Elikara herself explains some of it to Aeson during their last conversation, just before her Graduation. Because she is being deployed immediately, Aeson assumes she's with the Star Pilot Corps.

Elikara explains that it's actually not the SPC but a special mission with the **Imperial Fleet**.

Aeson finds this both fascinating and suspicious. He immediately starts to wonder what's going on—what Imperial Fleet Mission? What is his Father up to?

After he learns her tragic fate (what Xelio calls "some kind of *varqood* accident"), Aeson tries to force his Imperial Father into an explanation.

But Romhutat Kassiopei reveals very little. It was a **classified IF mission**, he tells his son. They were sent on a mission. **It failed.** The details of their unfortunate circumstances are not for public consumption. It is regrettable.

Aeson is *not* cleared to know any more. Except, mad with grief, he insists, asking where they were sent.

And the Imperator admits they were sent to *Earth*, on an **advance reconnaissance mission,** and it failed. This is all; Aeson is to tell no one, especially not Vekahat.

"Now, swear to me you will not speak of what I just told you and under no circumstances will you mention Earth."

This is the first inkling that Aeson has of the upcoming Earth Mission in which he will eventually take part along with so many others.

So, what exactly was this unfortunate advance scout mission? How did Elikara and her father die? What were they doing?

More answers will come in future novellas and novels of the series.

Ark-Ship Layout

When the Qualified Earth teens are taken up to the ark-ships, they are faced with immense confusing spaces filled with corridors, decks, and levels.

At some point we finally leave the shuttle bay and are taken through mind-blowingly endless hallways opening into decks and then into more convoluted passages with pale walls etched with ancient looking linear designs of hair-thin gold, beautiful and austere. The ship appears to be immense, so I lose track of any direction very quickly.

They must familiarize themselves with the ship layout. A directory map schematic can be called up at any display screen, and each of the ark-ships is identical.

The captains of each ark-ship give an introductory address to the Earth passengers, providing general information about the ship, the various decks and their functions, the living quarters and barracks, the meal halls, the medical sections, the exercise and recreation decks, the classrooms and training centers, the hydroponics and greenhouses, resonance chamber hubs and various ship systems, storage areas and shuttle bays.

The Earth Mission ark-ships have the following standard layout.

Each great "saucer" ark-ship is a **flattened sphere**. The circle is split into **four sections** from the center, a cross-cut forming four large "pie slices," and each "pie slice" or wedge is allocated to a **Quadrant**.

Yes, that's where that whole "Four Quadrant" notion comes from—four major divisions of function and labor on each of their ships! And, apparently this tradition has been in place for thousands of years, stemming from the time of their original colonization.

There are **four shuttle bays** in each ship, and they run lengthwise, almost the entire radius length of the ship, effectively making those four cross-cut "lines" that separate each Quadrant wedge.

In the circular heart of the ship, in the very center, is a great spherical chamber called the **Resonance Chamber**, very important for various systems functionality including actual propulsion and flight.

If the ark-ship were an egg, then the Resonance Chamber can be thought of as the yolk in the middle.

Each Quadrant wedge is cut across horizontally into **three sections**. The first and innermost smallest section of the wedge, adjacent to the central Resonance Chamber, is the **Command Deck**, the section where the **Atlantean Officers Quarters** are located, and where much of the ship control takes place.

The second, middle portion of the wedge, larger and closer to the outside, is the **Cadet Deck**. This is where the Cadets living quarters and training area is located.

Finally, the outermost largest section, number three, is the **Residential Deck**. This is where all the Civilians are housed, and it is adjacent to the **storage**, **hydroponics**, and other large-scale general **life support systems** areas closest to the outside hull.

The outermost feature is the **Observation Deck** which consists of a hall walkway that runs in a circle along the perimeter of the hull and has many large windows for watching the space panorama outside. It is often used for jogging exercise and relaxation.

That's the basic breakdown. There are many sub-levels and many corridors connecting the whole thing.

Earth Mission Ark-Ship Schematic

The Ark-Ship Environment

Gwen experiences her first moments on board an ark-ship with a visceral awareness.

> Neutral lukewarm air hits us with a blast. . . . No smell, all is clean, sterile. And yet, somehow I know beyond doubt I am breathing *alien* air onboard a spaceship—in its nothingness there's a hint of otherness, a *scent of the stars*.

However, there's nothing unusual about the gravity, and it feels just as though they are back on Earth, inside a vast depot. Except, everything is pristine cream and off-white, the gleaming hull lined with occasional panels of grey material with gold flecks that must be orichalcum.

The newly arrived Earth teens are overwhelmed. And then they have to deal with shuttle bays, endless ship corridors, crowded barracks filled with bunk beds, strange lavatory facilities, meal halls, and more, as described in the opening chapters of **Compete**.

Levels and Decks

The various ship decks and levels are stacked like pancakes and accessible via corkscrew stairwells and in some cases, service elevators.

✦ Level One – Main Ship Level

Everything the Earth refugees experience initially is located on the same **main ship level**—Command, Cadet, Residential Decks, the central hub with the Resonance Chamber, the space observation deck, et cetera. It is never specifically named but it is Level One.

However, they eventually have to go down to *lower* levels.

The only other levels described by Gwen are Levels Five, Six, and Seven.

✦ **Level Two** – unspecified, may be described in later novellas or
novels.

✦ **Level Three** – unspecified, may be described in later novellas
or novels.

✦ **Level Four** – unspecified, may be described in later novellas or
novels.

✦ **Level Five** – the **Interrogation Deck** and **Incarceration Deck**
This is a secure level, accessible only via key access card.
There is a long and dimly lit corridor. Rows of doors fill both
sides of the corridor. Two sets of guards patrol slowly down its length.
To enter past any given door, one needs to swipe a key card over a
secure panel next to it.

The rooms are small, dimly lit. One whole wall is a one-way
observation window into a brightly lit small cell—an interrogation
room.

When Gwen asks what else is down here, she is told that some
of it is auxiliary storage, and some of it includes places for keeping
prisoners—an incarceration deck. She also smells acrid smoke and
burning fumes coming from another level below (Level Six), and is
told there are *incinerators* there. The incinerators are accessible via a
special service elevator that's located next to the stairwell, and are
used, among other things, to dispose of the dead.

✦ **Level Six** – the **Manufacturing Deck** and the **Incinerators**
It's a large area, although much smaller than Hydroponics,
still an impressive warehouse of machinery and materials. Rows of
industrial 3D printers line the walls, and rows of various organic and
artificial raw "ink" materials fill storage containers up to the ceiling.

Atlantean crew members move about, working the machines.
Levitating robot vehicles transport boxes around from one pallet to
another.

There is also a smaller office enclosure where crew members and Earth refugees may enter specific printer programs into consoles.

The accessible systems contain, among other things, a huge library of Earth and Atlantean fashion, historical and modern. Most of it already resides in the Fleet Network Cloud.

✦ Level Seven – the Hydroponics Deck

Going down many flights down a corkscrew stairwell, one emerges in a glassed hallway which walls off a great open space, brightly lit with daylight illumination.

On the other side of the glass is a green oasis. Trees and shrubs and climbing vines fill a greenhouse that spans the entire length and width of the ark-ship. Earth plants mingle with what appears to be strange alien Atlantean vegetation. They hang suspended from special support beams overhead, into shallow troughs or deep containers of running water, their roots growing directly in the water without any soil.

The water contains a perfect balance of nutrients and chemicals necessary for growth. And it flows abundantly everywhere, including sprinklers and mist delivery systems.

Hydroponics is the deck that provides the ark-ship with food, oxygen, and other things necessary for life support. It is the largest and most vital of the general systems, and the H-Deck makes up the entirety of the ship on Level Seven.

Its ceiling stretches about seventy feet to accommodate most common varieties of trees.

Fun Fact: Both Sewage and Recycling systems are *shared* between Levels Six and Seven. Raw sewage and trash are processed on Six, then the separated and purified components are flushed down to Seven to be recycled and incorporated into the Hydroponics system.

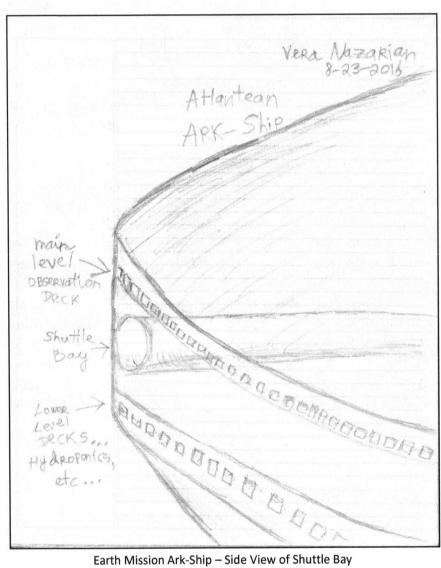

Earth Mission Ark-Ship – Side View of Shuttle Bay

Atlantean Shuttle Flight Instructions

HOW TO FLY AN ATLANTEAN SHUTTLE

Complete Step-By-Step Instructions

1) **Key yourself** to the console, console is activated.

2) Turn shuttle **on** with ready lights enabled by touching the **underside** of the console. *(Window shields will come open automatically revealing viewport.)*

3) The main **Pilot** sings **Major keying sequence** (3 notes) while holding down the four-color **ignition key** (raised bump on bottom center of console with four-color lights racing in a circle around each other). **Co-Pilot** repeats same steps, in order to be keyed to shuttle. *(Shuttle comes alive, is activated. Low harmonic hum in hull. Hair-fine threads of golden light race around the etchings on the hull.)*

4) Call up various Grids. **Propulsion** (top) / **Brake** (bottom). **Adjustment** (top) / **Navigation** (bottom). Tap any **corner** to switch to that grid. Tap **twice** to make it go **3D**.

5) While in **Yellow Grid**, set **Destination**. Swipe to the side next to the corner. *(Secondary smaller grid appears, with rows of Atlantean symbols.)*

6) Select first top left **circle character**—this ship, the **Home** button. Next to it, 4-point star *(astroctadra)* is the **Fleet Menu**.

7) **Tap Fleet Menu**, scroll up or down to **select destination ship**. *(Menu Grid disappears, two circles pop up on Navigation Grid.)*

8) **Pilot** calls up **Red Propulsion** Grid. Sings **major key sequence**. *(Hull vibration increases, shuttle leaves platform goes into launch channel.)*

9) **Co-Pilot** calls up **Blue Grid**, sings **minor key sequence**, manipulates **adjustments** to keep circle straight and centered along vertical line.

10) **Pilot** taps **Red twice** to go **3D**. Sings again. *(Shuttle starts moving.)*

11) **Pilot** swipes finger from center bottom outward to **increase speed**. *(Shuttle vibrates at higher pitch.)*

12) To **Brake**, **Co-Pilot** watches **Navigation Grid**, until the distance between **two circles** (Shuttle and Destination) is only one notch on vertical guide.

13) Tap **shuttle** circle **twice**, it signals **Brake** system. *(Circle starts blinking on Yellow Grid.)* *(Pilot's Red grid flashes and his circle flares bright red.)*

14) **Pilot** calls up **Green Grid**, holds down **Green** corner and swipes slowly **down** from top center to initiate **Brake**.

15) **Pilot** switches to **Red**, sings **turnabout sequence**, swiping finger in **circular motion** along middle of console. Same time, **Co-Pilot** on **Blue** continues to fine-tune.

16) **Pilot** switches to **Green** again to **Brake**. *(Shuttle coasts to a stop.)*

17) To **disengage** everything, press **ignition key**, sing same **3-note sequence** to turn **power off**. *(Hull goes dark and silent, shuttle parks and stops in place.)*

18) Power off each **console** by swiping **underside**.

19) Sing sequence to levitate console **back to wall** and **un-key** it.

Shuttle Weapons Grid

WEAPONS GRID

Partial Instructions

1) **Pilot** presses the **right** two corners – **Propulsion** (top) / **Brake** (bottom). At the same time, **Co-Pilot** presses the **left** two corners – **Adjustment** (top) / **Navigation** (bottom). *(White Grid activates. White circle is shuttle, other color circles indicate other vessels or objects.)*

The above instructions are incomplete because the actual firing of ship weapons via the use of the Weapons Grid has not been elaborated during Gwen's classes. However, these instructions may be referenced in detail in the prequel series *Dawn of The Atlantis Grail*, and some of the novellas and novels.

Quantum Stream Safety

The following safety instructions are taught to all the Cadets during Pilot Classes.

1. Do **not** under any circumstances breach the **Boundary** demarcation of the **Quantum Stream** zone.
2. Maintain your **flight course**. Adhere to **straight lines**.
3. **Avoid** making **sudden sharp movements** or turns.
4. In case of **obstacles**, **slow down** first, then engage in **evasive maneuvers**.
5. **Brake earlier** than normal.
6. **Surrender right of way** to any other ship in your immediate vicinity if they are **too close** to the **QS Boundary**, allowing them to stay inside the Stream.

7. If you have the misfortune to **Breach** and fall **outside** the **QS Boundary**, follow the *QS Breach Emergency Protocol*, or *QSBEP-1*.

The Quantum Stream Breach Emergency Protocol

The following instructions on how to react in case of an emergency Breach are posted inside every shuttle, in a highly visible spot near the Pilot console.

However, they are intended more as a cautionary warning, and considered practically meaningless. For all practical purposes, almost no one can ever *return*—get back inside the Quantum Steam after an accidental Breach.

QSBEP-1 Emergency Instructions

1. **Listen** to the space around you in all directions for any QS signal trace.
2. **Sing** the **exact frequency** to match **quantum resonance** until shuttle acknowledges the match and is keyed. **Synch** the shuttle to the **QS field**.
3. **Plot** the signal **coordinates** onto the **Navigation Grid**.
4. Set new course and **pursue the QS field** immediately.
5. **Re-enter** the **Quantum Stream** zone as soon as you are within reach.

The Four Color Quadrants Cube

CHAPTER 14 – Military: Ships, Fleet Structure, Weapons

The military tradition is ancient and honorable on Atlantis. Since the colony planet settlers are space-faring, most of the military is organized in national Fleets local to each country, and the most basic military rank across the board is that of Pilot.

The Earthie Choice: Fleet Cadet or Civilian

When the Qualified Earth refugees are first taken up to the ark-ships, they are instructed to make an early life choice: become a Fleet Cadet or a Civilian.

"What does this mean for you?" Commander Manakteon Resoi continues. "It means, you have to decide *now* how you will spend the rest of your lives.

The military Fleet offers more privileges and advantages, including higher rank, higher education, and higher pay even after retirement. But it also demands so much more from those who enlist, up to and including their life. It is not for everyone. In fact, it is not for the great majority of the Earth refugees.

Meanwhile, the Earth refugees who choose a Civilian life—which most do—will have access to education and various trades, and to solid basics. More details will be provided, to assist them with making their final selection.

They have five days to make this life decision, after which, there will be no going back. They will be assigned to their permanent place on the Atlantean ark-ships for the rest of this journey, according to their Quadrant and final rank designation, and they will begin their duties and their in-depth education.

Fleet Structure

Cadets enroll in the **Fleet Cadet School** at the age of seven, and spend four years studying. At the end of year one, the *kefarai* newbie Cadets declare their Color Quadrant affiliation and participate in the Quadrant Choosing Ceremony. By the end of their four years of schooling they make the decision of remaining in their country's national **Fleet** or joining the international **Star Pilot Corps**.

After graduation, they are assigned the basic rank of **Pilot** (lowest being **Third Rank**), and stationed at various Fleet locations.

With sufficient years of service and accomplishments, Pilots advance in Rank from **Third** to **Second**, to **First**. After attaining **First Rank**, Pilots are eligible for positions of Command. They may become **Captains** of their assigned vessels.

Captains can also command *formation groupings of vessels*, starting from small **Pinions** of vessels, to larger **Wings**, then entire **Waves**.

These formations are usually divided into Color Quadrants, such as:

Red Pinion
Blue Pinion
Green Pinion
Yellow Pinion

Red Wing
Blue Wing
Green Wing
Yellow Wing

Red Wave
Blue Wave
Green Wave
Yellow Wave

There is also a unique rear formation called **Shuut (Feather/Tail)** which consists of specialized ships, usually carrying civilian VIPs and wartime correspondents, that are capable of escape at a moment's notice. The *Shuut* can also perform other non-standard tasks on behalf of the Fleet during battle.

Pinions are the smallest of formations and are most often made up of solo fighter *mafdets*, and two-Pilot *ardukats*. Wings of multiple Pinions are larger, more complex formations, most often holding four Pinions per Wing (one for each Quadrant), and several four-Pilot *khepri* in charge, flying in the vanguard position. Waves contain multiple Wings and usually execute very complex maneuvers, and are populated with all types of light-duty fighter vessels, with heavy *ankhurats* in command, flying vanguard. Note that *sebasarets* normally do not participate in normal formation warfare, but wait outside the battle zone. Likewise, battle barges wait beyond the battle theater, having launched all the smaller ships.

Some formation groupings are assigned **Leaders** by the Captain or greater commanding officer. For example, a **Pinion Leader** is a Pilot chosen to perform specific *mission maneuvers* and direct the other fighter vessels in that formation, during that mission only.

In larger military vessels, there are multiple Pilots, usually in charge of the Four Quadrants divisions in each ship and led by a single Captain. The Four Quadrant Pilots of large vessels work together in the **Resonance Chamber**, executing voice commands for primary navigation and weapons discharge.

Captains who have earned *special distinctions* or who are in charge of *multiple* large military vessels are **Command Pilots**.

The Command Pilot in charge of the entire Fleet is called the **Commander**.

National Fleets on Atlantis

The following is a list of major nations and their national Fleets. These country-specific Fleets have significant numbers and large classes of vessels, advanced weapons capability, and sufficient numbers of highly trained personnel to wage major warfare.

Lesser nations without significant organized Fleets and with only small armed forces at their disposal (in the form of regional guards and militias), are not listed below.

Imperial *Atlantida* – Imperial Fleet
New Deshret – Pharikonei Fleet
Ubasti – National Fleet
Eos-Heket – Republic Fleet
Vai Naat – Crown Fleet
Ptahleon – Helios Fleet
Shuria – Lower Fleet
Bastet – Niktos Fleet

Star Pilot Corps (SPC)

In addition to the various country-specific national fleets, Atlantis the colony planet has an international space force in charge of planetary defense.

The Atlantean Fleet—as a military *institution* in its grander sense—has **two** primary functions—first, as a ***national defense force*** to protect its home nation from military hostilities from other countries here on Atlantis, and second, a ***global force*** to protect this planet from alien threats.

In case of Imperial *Atlantida*, the former is the **Imperial Fleet**, loyal to its nation, while the latter is the Fleet's special dedicated branch called **Star Pilot Corps** whose loyalty lies to the entire planet. When a Cadet joins the military (any national fleet), they can choose to specialize in one or the other. But the first step is always their local national fleet.

The Imperial Fleet is the armed forces of Imperial *Atlantida*. Other countries have their own local Fleet equivalents. Ubasti has the National Fleet, Eos-Heket has the Republic Fleet, New Deshret, has the *Pharikonei* Fleet, and so on.

All these Fleets offer their top Pilots the option to also apply for the Star Pilot Corps which is a special program that crosses national boundaries. Pilots from different countries attend an intensive series of advanced courses and spend time training in space. They train all around Hel's system, on orbiting stations around the system planets such as Ishtar Station, Tammuz Station, and Septu Station—these three being largest—and many others.

Star Pilot Corps is all up in orbit or in deep space. Even the **SPC Central Command Headquarters** is located on a station in Atlantis orbit. There is no formal ground-based SPC operations office *anywhere* on the surface of Atlantis. It's done in order to preserve the international flavor of the program and to maintain the equality and power dynamics of all nations.

The command structure is also separate, with minor overlap. While Manakteon Resoi is the Commander of the Imperial Fleet (and as such, in charge of the Earth Mission, primarily Imperial *Atlantida's* enterprise), he holds a lesser rank of Command Pilot of one of the battle barges (War-1) in the Star Pilot Corps. Meanwhile, while Aeson Kassiopei is only a Command Pilot in the Imperial Fleet, second in command to the IF Commander, he happens to be the senior commanding officer of the Star Pilot Corps—SPC Commander. When it comes to matters of *planetary defense*, all national fleet Commanders defer to the SPC Commander.

Note that no country's primary leader may serve as the SPC Commander, since it constitutes a conflict of interest too large to surmount. For example, as soon as Aeson Kassiopei becomes Imperator he steps down from his SPC Commander position.

At present there are **240,000 personnel** in the SPC Fleet.

Astra Daimon

The **astra daimon** are a self-chosen, informal brotherhood and sisterhood of the most outstanding Pilots in the Star Pilot Corps—the best of the best. They are the elite of the SPC, who have mastered their disciplines and excelled beyond the highest expectations of their rank.

The *astra daimon* answer to no one but their own. You cannot join, you may only be chosen. To be chosen as one of them, a Pilot must earn the honor. A candidate for inclusion must be nominated by one or more of the current *astra daimon* and then voted upon. The details of this process are kept secret. Similarly, much of the rest of what goes on is hidden from outsiders.

The *astra daimon* have mastered the disciplines of at least one of the Four Quadrants and are proficient in all. The wearing of one's Quadrant armband has deeper meaning to the *daimon*. These are not mere "affiliation colors" but a symbol of their chosen discipline and Allegiance to the Quadrant.

The term *astra daimon* literally means "star demon."

You have been called out by one of your peers and you must answer.

Pilot Call Signs

The following call signs have been mentioned in the series. Call signs are codename and nickname identifiers of specific Pilots or special mission members. They are used during military operations to simplify communication and maintain a layer of anonymity for security purposes.

Phoebos – Aeson Kassiopei
Bast – Oalla Keigeri
Sobek – Keruvat Ruo
Shamash – Xelio Vekahat
Tefnut – Erita Qwas
Lark – Gwen Lark
Ixion – Quoni Enutat
Nepht – Unspecified pilot in Red Pinion
Babi – Unspecified pilot in Red Pinion
Imeier (followed by number) – special ops position call sign of the *Pegasei* Release Team (PRT) unit captain of the *Pegasei* Retrieval Khenneb Mission.
Onyx (followed by number) – position call signs of other PRT unit operators of *Pegasei* Retrieval Khenneb Mission.

Er-Du Martial Arts

Outside of the formal military, a universal form of *individual* combat training is **Er-Du**, an ancient martial art system reminiscent of Earth's Kung Fu and Tai Chi traditions, a combination of hard work and personal achievement in honing the mind-body energy balance.

Philosophy and Fundamental Purpose

Aeson's meaningful response to Gwen's question as to "why must there be Combat" in **Qualify**, Chapter 8, summarizes the underlying philosophy:

"In Atlantis, we believe in taking responsibility for ourselves. As you learn to fight, you learn to defend yourself from physical harm. You acquire a powerful self-preserving skill set, and a specific attitude. This attitude carries across to other aspects of your life. So that you can defend yourself from other *less tangible* but far more dangerous things that can break you—not just your body, but your spirit. Things such as deception, corruption, disparagement, coercion, false accusation and persecution. Subtle evil things that undermine *you*. And if you can maintain the inner ability to defend yourself against influence, you can build a *purpose* in your life that no one can take away from you.

"In Atlantis, we believe that purpose is the most important virtue. You can lose your freedom, your health, your honor, everything you love and care about. And yet, if you still have your purpose, you have lost nothing."

During Qualification on Earth, the Candidates are introduced to the art of combat and taught the Twelve Forms of this ancient tradition.

Er-Du Forms (Fundamental Twelve)

Forms of Er-Du (Fundamental Twelve)		
Form 1	**Floating Swan**	Resting position, used to begin and end a traditional sparring bout.
Form 2	**Striking Snake**	Focused intense strikes.
Form 3	**Spinning Wind**	Fast spin, light evasive motion.
Form 4	**Spinning Water**	Slow spin, high force strike.
Form 5	**Bristling Fish**	Low crouch, strike as you rise.
Form 6	**Flowing Fire**	Rapid hand strike volley.
Form 7	**Running Scarab**	Shielding defensive motion to imitate the scarab beetle rolling dung.
Form 8	**Kicking Horse**	Roundhouse kicks, with or without back-flip combo.
Form 9	**Weaving Spider**	Yellow Quadrant specialty, medium crouch, complex finger motion, with or without the use of net and cord weapons.
Form 10	**Cutting Fang**	Red Quadrant specialty, using sharp rings and other concealed palm and knuckle weapons.
Form 11	**Shooting Star**	Blue Quadrant specialty, using throw weapons such as sharpened *astroctadra* stars, darts, and other needle projectiles.
Form 12	**Shielding Stone**	Green Quadrant specialty, using defensive bucklers and weaponizing otherwise non-weapon everyday objects.

Many of the Forms are intended to work in pairs, naturally complementing each other like "yin and yang" opposites, so that one Form serves as attack and the other works as best defense against the first one. An example of common *natural form pairing* is Striking Snake (attack) paired with Running Scarab (defense).

In addition to natural form pairing, all "attack" Forms can be used to **actively defend** against any other attack forms. Here, self-defense is achieved by means of offense—a basic counter-attack.

A student of Er-Du learns all **possible combinations of form interactions and pairing**, and becomes proficient in both natural pairs and general (random) pairing matchups. This way, the student can anticipate and choose which Form serves best in any given situation against an opponent.

The *Primary Twelve Forms* cycle is a practice exercise wherein the students go through all the Twelve Forms in order, and then start again from the beginning, repeating continuously, until they are told to stop by the Instructor. This is one intensive method of practice to attain proficiency.

Limited Mobility Forms of Er-Du

In addition to the twelve standard forms, advanced Combat training is continued in **Limited Mobility Forms** or **LM Forms**, intended to allow soldiers who have been incapacitated to continue fighting. Knowing this skill set can mean the difference between survival and death on the battlefield.

These additional advanced Forms have evolved for a vital reason. Wounded soldiers need a means of supporting their injured, variously incapacitated bodies while continuing to fight. The LM Forms of Er-Du are taught to all in the Fleet as part of basic training, because they are necessary. Limited Mobility is an honorable aspect of military training for an Atlantis warrior. Every soldier experiences it at some point, and it consistently saves lives.

When Aeson trains Blayne Dubois in the use of his hoverboard in combination with LM Forms, he demonstrates the importance of this advanced technique.

In this context, the hoverboard itself serves a dual purpose—as the basis for mobility, and as a defensive shield. There are three fundamental LM Forms involved:

First LM Shield Form	Using your **lower limbs** as much as possible to keep the hoverboard anchored and covering you while you fight with your upper body.
Second LM Shield Form	Combination of **lower limbs** and using **only one upper limb** at a time to position it to your advantage (wounded shoulder, severed limb) to block your opponent, while **one hand fights**. Particularly important when a soldier only has the use of one hand.
Third LM Shield Form	Uses **both hands to hold the board** while your lower body makes **no contact** with it at all—requires a great deal of upper body strength to support your own weight entirely while you manipulate the board as a shield. Basically, you are hanging off the board in an upright position as dead weight and moving it too. A severely disadvantaged position, last resort defense.

Grip of Friendship

This is a special emergency rescue technique when on a hoverboard or anywhere you have to support or carry another person in *mid-air*. Useful if the subject is unable to act, is hanging on by their hands, and it's only up to *you* to help them—when you can only reach and grab them by one hand. The rescuer reaches out with one hand, underneath, to firmly clasp the other's arm above the wrist, so that the insides of your arms touch. Both of you hold the other's arm *above* the wrist. This hold is similar to that of trapeze artists when they hold each other with arms and hands alone as they swing. It can save your life, and prevent a fall. No other mutual hold or grip is as secure as this one.

Military Salutes

Cadets are taught several specific Salute Forms as part of their Er-Du training. Salutes are a sign of respect and honor. These are not to be confused with the *standard military salute* used in the Fleet.

The four-part **Form Salute** is the one taught back on Earth before the Qualification Semi-Finals. It consists of a series of full-body movements and is supposed to be the brief form of the ancient Er-Du Salute given during formal Combat. Cadets have not yet been taught the full extended Form—that's a lesson for another class year.

Form Salute of *Atlantida*, Long Form, Short Form

The ancient **Form Salute** of *Atlantida* in Er-Du is sometimes referred to as the **Thirteenth Form**. The Salute is done as a sign of respect to one's equal or superior.

At the early stage of Er-Du training, all Cadets salute only their Instructors and each other. Before each sparring session, each sparring partner salutes their honorable opponent. However—one does not salute an opponent who has exhibited a lack of honor. And one does not salute one's *inferiors*. This is not intended as a slight but to ensure fair matchups between formal opponents.

By definition, "your inferiors are those who have no training to match yours." This applies to any field, not only Er-Du. In the special and somewhat unusual case of Earth Cadets, their inferiors on Atlantis are most native non-citizens, even though all Earthies are also categorized under a non-citizen immigrant status.

The Salute Form (Short Version)

The brief Form of the Er-Du Salute consists of four elements.

1. Step to the side with your right foot, widening your stance. At the same time bring two fists together, knuckles touching, arms bent at chest-level.

2. Open fists, palms facing out. Touch the tip of the thumb and index finger of one hand to the corresponding digits on your other hand, so that the empty space between the two hands forms a triangle.

3. Bring your two palms together as if praying, but keep thumbs at a ninety-degree angle from other fingers. Draw the "praying" hands toward you, so the thumbs touch your chest. At the same time incline your head so that the fingertips touch your forehead. Maintain the wide stance and bent knees.

4. Separate the hands, lifting them outward into a circular sweeping arc, and return them palms down at your sides. As you straighten, bring the right leg back in, ending with feet together.

The Atlantean Fleet Military Salute

The Fleet Salute is very simple, performed with the left hand and involving lips and forehead. It is done to show respect to one's superior commanding officers.

1. Incline head slightly.

2. Raise left hand, placing palm against forehead while keeping your fingers and thumb open at a ninety-degree angle.

3. Quickly slide your palm down and turn it so that your fingertips are now touching the forehead, and your thumb is touching your lips.

Other Salutes and Curtseys

During Court Protocol lessons, Gwen is taught to make a formal Atlantean high-ranking woman's greeting, which is a form of a curtsey and salute combined. The details of this are not specified. It involves making the gestures of the military salute with the left hand, at the same time lowering oneself in a bowing stance with the right foot placed before the left foot and angled.

Mafdet

Ardukat

Khepri

Ankhwat

War

Atlantean Military Fleet Vessels

Fleet Vessels

The following is a description of each type of ship mentioned in the series.

War – also known as a battle barge, or battle barge-caliber battleship. Only ten battle barges exist, numbered 1-10, with the first being the most distinguished flagship, and then diminishing in reputation and resources with each numbered designation. This is the biggest warship class in the SPC Fleet, with 24,000 personnel capacity (the equivalent of four ark-ships), and four times bigger in size because it has to transport hundreds of other warships inside, including 100 large *sebasarets* (which are filled in turn with mid-range transport *depets* such as velo-cruisers, small fighters, and more). When a battle barge carries the SPC Fleet Commander it gets the temporary designation of *Depet-Ra* (similar to Air Force One, the airplane of the US President on Earth). Once the Commander leaves, that battle barge is again simply called a War. Following the tradition of a long-standing strategic assumption that threats will appear from outside the system, the most high-powered and prestigious battle barges are assigned to patrol the outer system.

 The following are the permanent locations of each battle barge stationed in the Helios System, shown starting from innermost proximity to Helios and all the way to the outermost gas giants:

Helios	☼	[Alien Enemy ships emerge here, defying all expectations]
Rah	o	War-10
Septu	o	War-9
Tammuz	o	War-8
Ishtar	o	War-7
Atlantis	o	War-5, War-6
Olympos	o	War-3, War-4
Atlas	o	War-1, War-2

Sebasaret – large midrange military transport, not considered a fighter. A command ship carrier for ranking officers, military personnel, and other vessels. Can be used as transport and command center, and for science research in addition to military deployment. Has weapons capability, but no guns, only guided missiles. Different combinations of fighter ships can fit inside. Its fighter bay is designed to hold the following combinations:

       * four ankhurats.
       * two ankhurats, four khepri.
       * four *khepri*, eight *ardukats*.
       * eight *ardukats*, twelve *mafdets*.

Velocity Cruiser (Velo-Cruiser) – 25-person capacity, small to midrange, high-speed civilian transport, halfway between an *ankhurat* and a *khepri* in size.

Transport Shuttle – 100-passenger capacity, plus two pilots. Common civilian transport, was used on Earth during Qualification to transport Candidates to the Semi-Finals and Finals.

Shuttle – 7-person capacity, standard seven-seat civilian transport, slightly larger than an *ardukat*.

Solo Shuttle – civilian solo transport, the same size as a *mafdet*. Used for beginner training of Fleet Cadets.

Mafdet – solo fighter, 2 guns, front and back, fine focused plasma bursts for strafing, nicknamed "The Needle of Justice."

Ardukat – 2-crew fighter, 4 guns, fine-focus burst and wide scatter-burst, Pilot and Co-Pilot flight pair. The most common small combat ship in the Fleet.

Khepri – 4-crew fighter with 4 spinning spiral guns, heavy-caliber artillery, higher density plasma, multiple thick nozzles, 4 guided missiles and armed probes. This is an attack bomber for major targets. **Ankhurat** – 100-crew fighter and military transport vessel, plus 6 Pilots, 6 heavy-caliber plasma guns, and 10 missiles. Intended for boarding other vessels. Nicknamed "Ankh, the Life Giver."

Khopesh (sickle sword) – an ancient type of fighter vessel, introduced in the prequel series *Dawn of the Atlantis Grail*.

Shamshir – another variety of ancient fighter vessel, introduced in the prequel series.

Onyx Claw – ancient squadron formation introduced in the prequel series.

Helios System Station Nomarchs and SPC Commanders

Atlas Station
Station Nomarch **Dythrat**
War-1 – Command Pilot **Manakteon Resoi** (Imperial Atlantida)
War-2 – Command Pilot **Amaiar Uluatl** (New Deshret)

Olympos Station
Station Nomarch **Yelen**
War-3 – Command Pilot **Chudo Batiaxaat** (Ubasti)
War-4 – Command Pilot **Saiva Neidos** (Eos-Heket)

Atlantis Station/Star Pilot Corps Headquarters
Station Nomarch **Evandros**
War-5 – Command Pilot **Selmiris Teth** (Vai Naat)
War-6 – Command Pilot **Uru Onophris** (Ptahleon)

Ishtar Station
Station Nomarch **Danaat**
War-7 – Command Pilot **Mayavat Meropei** (Shuria)

Tammuz Station
Station Nomarch **Cretheo**
War-8 – Command Pilot **Lafaoh Ungreb** (Bastet)

Septu Station
Station Nomarch **Asclep**
War-9 – Command Pilot **Saramana Zhar** (Qurartu)

Rah Station
Station Nomarch **Rertu**
War-10 – Command Pilot **Eodea Tecpatl** (Ankh-Tawi, Weret, combined forces)

CHAPTER 15 – The Aliens

The reader first learns about the existence of the terrible and mysterious "They" in **Compete**, when Gwen discovers the existence of the holographic ark-ship, and from that moment on, the stakes in the story are suddenly raised.

"They"—the Ancient Enemy, the Aliens of the Golden Light

Until the nameless aliens finally appear in **Survive**, they are referred to as the "ancient enemy" in the series. Not much is known about them at all, it seems, not even by the Imperial Kassiopei or their loyal and erudite priesthood.

When the destructive golden lights appear around Hel and start destroying space stations around the Helios system, they are "recognized" by everyone and assumed to be the same ancient enemy who drove them to flee Earth in the first place.

Legends, myths, and traditional children's stories on the colony planet Atlantis speak of a **Starlight Sorceress** who had some kind of **magic enemy**—an *evil star*, or a ghost made of golden light—that didn't want to listen or play with her, unlike the others (various companion animals). These stories have a basis in historical reality and memories of the real ancient enemy.

When *they* actually appear for the first time, it is revealed that *they* are *astroctadra* shapes of blinding golden light, hanging in space. At first it is unclear whether these shapes are their natural physical forms or just their spaceships. However, the revelations continue as the aliens materialize inside the ship and make themselves known to Gwen, Aeson, and the others.

Each alien being arrives as a **disembodied golden *sun***, about a meter in diameter, and takes up space, floating in the air before the humans. It fluctuates and spins around its axis, sending forth waves of plasma like small armlets that grow longer with each swirl, until it reshapes into a vaguely **humanoid form**, standing up seven or eight feet tall, its head nearly touching the ceiling. It has no face, no features, no mouth or eyes, only light.

In addition to **Thoth**, the other beings name themselves **Set, Isis,** and **Horus**.

They reveal the true nature of the golden light spheres forming around Helios and the various space stations in the system. It is **OSIRIS**, an ancient automated program of mass destruction on a grand star system scale.

OSIRIS powers itself by the solar energy of the very star which it is set to destroy. It's a brute force method of planetary cleansing, created and activated by the aliens 12,500 years ago in response to humanity's handling of the harmful quantum dimensional rift that the humans opened on Earth in ancient times.

The Origin and Purpose of Humanity

The aliens of the golden spheres and the automated OSIRIS destruction program—known to the ancients as the gods of Egypt, among others—claim to have merely *discovered* Earth and its resident humanity. According to them, they do not know who "made" humanity.

But they claim to know humanity's *purpose*, having watched the human evolution taking place over the millennia. Supposedly it is the same for all sentient species starting out.

What, then, is humanity's purpose?

According to the aliens, humanity's *purpose* is to *support each other* as we advance into eternity. Instead of consuming each other, we must nourish. Instead of abusing the non-sentient animal species that share our worlds, we must care for, steward, and protect them.

Evaluation and Judgement of Humanity

There are certain criteria by which the aliens evaluate humanity and their fitness as a sentient species.

> The ultimate sign of a stable sentient civilization is the ability to create, wield, or recognize entanglement with *any other* particle in the universe by reaching out with *love* and making a connection.

The definition of love used here is the *recognition* of *self* in the *other*, a sense of affinity.

> A second indicator of mature sentience is the ability to safely pass through the universal fabric and the infinite constructs of reality at a quantum level without disturbing its equilibrium or ripping it apart.

Thus, the ancient notion of traversing the universe on a Ship of Eternity is the ultimate expectation of a fully sentient species.

What exactly does it mean? The prequel series **Dawn of the Atlantis Grail** explores this in depth.

It comes down to the penetration of **membranes**, boundaries, limits.

The ability to travel across dimensions and universes should be a smooth, gentle, seamless transition—by means of changing quantum states to match and effortlessly passing across membranes—not a forceful intrusion, or a destructive physical phenomenon that creates an imbalance in the quantum system (such as the ancient *quantum dimensional rift*).

According to the aliens, spacetime is an immense illusion, defined by limits, boundaries, and membranes—a *grand construct* made of infinite lesser ones. And each "lesser construct" is merely another enclosed subsystem with its own single branch of *cause and effect*. In other words, each system's energy output and chains of consequences are spawned from a single origin point (a singularity, such as the Big Bang) and apply only along that one dimension.

What about Deity?

The aliens themselves are *not* gods. Nor do they claim to be. The "they" aliens are merely *something more*, something that humanity is not.

According to the being called *Horu...th* or Horus:

> *"As such, we were unto gods once, to your ancient Earth peoples—teaching them complex realities perceived as wonders—but we do not presume. Nor do we want the worship."*

Thus, in the end of the core series, it is revealed that these superior beings were ultimately deified by humanity—as gods of Egypt, gods of Atlantis, and many more, going way back into the past. But they are not the original creators who seeded the planet.

Then, who or what did?

More answers are coming in the prequel series *Dawn of the Atlantis Grail*!

Pegasei

The other important alien species in the series are the *pegasei*, a quantum, *trans-dimensional* life form.

Originally considered to be an **inferior and non-sentient alien species** by the general public, the *pegasei* are treated as exotic animals and kept as pets in quantum containment force field "cages" by affluent and influential humans—such as Lady Irana Nokut and her baby *pegasus* (a tiny energy blob of rainbow light) whom Gwen first encounters in the gardens of the Imperial Palace (**Win**, Chapter 8). Little is known about them except that they are *energy beings* that feed on *sunlight*, and perish if denied light energy.

According to Princess Manala, a *pegasus* "needs to move between dimensions to be properly healthy." However, according to a breeder who reassures Lady Irana, "regular exposure to direct sunlight is all the *pegasus* needs to survive."

The *pegasei* are used during the Games of the Atlantis Grail in the fourth Stage, and that's when Gwen discovers the stunning truth about their true nature.

The Contenders in Stage Four receive their *pegasei*. Each trans-dimensional creature is restrained and held inside an active quantum containment field sphere (an orb) that can be opened only *once* by means of a keying voice command. During the training portion, if they allow their *pegasus* to escape, become injured, or die, they are disqualified.

Some Contenders try to control their *pegasei* by isolating them in darkness—a cruelty, since the *pegasei* are deprived of sustenance.

Eventually the *pegasei* are harnessed.

After Gwen manages to harnesses her *pegasus*, she soon realizes that there is something odd happening—a kind of buzzing in her sinuses during certain musical notes.

The buzzing itch increases with some notes and decreases with others. She experiments with different notes, then suddenly feels a blast inside her mind—a blinding flash of ripping *pain* explodes in her forehead, its location deep under the skin in the middle spot above the bridge of her nose.

And then, like a tunnel, *something* opens. A flood of sensory data swirls through Gwen—images, colors, sounds, scents, immense stars and microscopic specks of sub-atomic particles.

Her world shifts. She perceives an alien *presence* within her mind, neither male nor female.

The being explains to Gwen that it is alien to her world and universe. However, its kind were brought into her space-time reality from the physical location of Earth.

Their species has a name, but the name humans gave them, together with this original form of fixed matter, is sufficient. They are *pegasei*.

She calls the being **Arion**, in honor of the wise sentient horse from Ancient Greek mythology.

Arion tells her that the unique frequency is a connection between her form of energy and his/her/its. Few humans are able to connect to *pegasei*. Those who do, they value. But they also ask for discretion because they are in constant danger from humans.

Arion explains that an exception has been made for her because of the nature of the situation and her own nature. It also reveals that once they are connected, all the *pegasei* everywhere can hear her.

When Gwen is unable to rest, closing her eyes, and still "hearing" the sensory data stream deep in her forehead, Arion tells her to breathe and let go, and that she must sleep.

Sleep is when you yourself become data.

Arion reveals that when one sleeps, one lets go, and is pulled back in through the link—the same opening that leads to the rest of the universe.

As the Game Stage progresses, and it's time for the final Triathlon Race, it is explained that the *pegasei* may not interfere with outcomes of events because they must maintain their disguise.

After the exciting race is over (and Gwen rides Arion, transformed in the shape of the fastest animal on Earth), she realizes she must let him go.

Arion tells her that it and the other *pegasei* will continue to be held in captivity, but that it trusts Gwen because it knows her now.

Gwen liberates Arion who explodes into a plasma light cloud, and is free.

Thank you. I am never too far from you. Remember the frequency. Think of me. . . .

The *pegasei* continue to play an important role in the story.

It is revealed that *pegasei* are somehow connected to the black hole Ae-Leiterra.

Aeson tells Gwen the events leading up to his death at Ae-Leiterra and then miraculous resurrection (**Survive**, chapter 21).

Black hole energy emissions are a common occurrence around the Rim of Ae-Leiterra. Particles of emitted **trans-dimensional energy** break out somehow from the gravitational pull, and alongside them, so do *pegasei*.

These trans-dimensional quantum beings seem to **literally appear out of nowhere**, somehow **escaping the gravitational pull** of the black hole.

They start moving outward along the Rim radius toward the exterior edge, where they gather in **massive super-flocks**. This happens gradually until the super-flocks are large enough to be **harvested**.

But, it's never about *pegasei*. It's about what their presence indicates.

The *Great Quantum Shield* at the Rim of Ae-Leiterra keeps trans-dimensional entities such as the ancient alien enemy out of this space-time. It keeps them from passing through the trans-dimensional wormhole pathways via the black hole.

Atlanteans have been taught throughout history that the alien enemy first came to Earth's Ancient Atlantis the same way as the *pegasei*.

If *pegasei* show up, the ancient alien enemy is soon to follow.

And now it appears that the *pegasei* are coming from the inadequately shielded Earth rift via a wormhole and ending up all the way across the universe, in Atlantis.

The Earth rift is leaking directly here!

The Imperator takes the Fleet on a maintenance mission to the Rim, after receiving reports from SPC Command about *pegasei* sightings.

During that fateful mission Aeson sacrifices himself for the Fleet in his Father's stead (and earns the **black armband** of a hero). He drives a shuttle beyond the decaying edge of the Shield Boundary, singing the required voice sequence, and sees a **small flock of pegasei**, seething in glorious rainbow colors among the fiery chaos of the Rim.

At this point, the tragedy happens. Aeson performs his selfless sacrifice and begins to die in the inferno of the accretion disk.

But then, somehow, he is ***brought back***.

They tell Aeson it was a miracle, a lucky fluke.

However, a ***pegasei* energy fluctuation** is recorded at the same time.

At that same exact moment, a flock completely engulfed the shuttle, and even appeared to accompany it just as the shuttle rebounded back into the SQS safe zone. Then the flock dissipated, as quickly as our instruments could register. It was almost as if they hadn't even been there. And neither was the shockwave.

The *pegasei* act to save Aeson when he is already *dead*.

Back on Atlantis, Aeson's body is rushed to Poseidon, taken out of stasis to prepare him for the final after-death process. And then, impossibly, **he wakes up on the work table slab**, surrounded by frightened and confused funeral techs.

Then, more events reveal how deeply the *pegasei* are involved in everything.

The ancient Princess **Arlenari Kassiopei's** personal **diary** is brought to light—a secret record she calls **The Book of Everything**— and the reader learns even more of their ancient involvement in the events 12,500 years ago, back on Earth (**Survive**, Chapter 82).

This entry in The Book of Everything explains the *pegasei* regularly emerging from the Great Quantum Shield at Ae-Leiterra.

They are ***entangled* with others of their kind** across the universe, between *here* and *there*. **They are keeping the rift open.**

In addition, Arlenari Kassiopei makes a comparison to the *pegasei* when she mentions her mysterious twin brother **Oron,** who, for unknown reasons, stays behind on Earth. As a result, he is disowned by the Imperial Kassiopei Dynasty, and his name stricken from all historical records.

Fun Fact: The ancient mythic Pegasus form—the physical construct of a winged horse—was created by the *pegasei* as a result of picking the minds of ancient humans. They combined different elements of different creatures to create a new shape.

Arlenari's diary describes the moment **she realized *pegasei* are sentient**. It's an interesting parallel to Gwen's own experience. It is also the moment that the Lark family understands the truth that *pegasei* are *sentient* aliens held against their will and not just cute rainbow animals—and just possibly, gods. Slavery, or trafficking of sentient beings is both unethical and *criminal*.

Gwen finally reveals what she knows, and surprisingly, so does Aeson and Manala.

Next, the Larks and Aeson attempt to **convince the Imperator and the others**. And the Imperator presents the urgent need to liberate the pegasei to the **IEC members and foreign heads of state**. Not only is it the ethical thing to do, but it just might save Atlantis.

The revelation is shocking to all.

They are like foreign shards left inside an open wound gushing in the fabric of space-time. They keep it from closing up and healing itself—which puts us forever in danger from this accursed quantum passageway. And the worst of it is—*we* placed them there!

How was this done? The ancient Atlanteans simply separated the *pegasei* from their own kind, **like pulling apart a ball of tacky glue**.

Except it was done with **quantum glue through a cosmic wormhole**. So now the wormhole is filled with the energetic strings of their quantum residue—the *pegasei* living essence stretched across the universe.

Numerous flocks of *pegasei* were taken by the reckless ancestors with them when they left Earth, by means of the ancient cosmic passage that originated in the dimensional rift on Earth.

The *pegasei* are all linked together, entangled at the quantum level. When even one of them is taken to the opposite end of the universe, it's like tying an unbreakable string from it to the others—quantum glue. **The entanglement acts to create a tunnel through space-time**. It's a **permanent link** between here and there—the ancient home world.

And then the sentience aspect is brought up.

Gwen uses the frequency to summon Arion.

Arion says that yes, now it is the right time. The pegasei have been waiting for all the elements to align.

It is a matter of liberating both the species—*pegasei* and human.

"Release us, and we will leave you and this part of the cosmos. As we travel back through the wormhole passage into the Earth rift, we will collect scattered parts of ourselves along the way, to recombine in our own universe. The rift will heal and close on its own. Your true enemy will abandon you to yourselves."

Arion adds that they cannot make an absolute promise, but the alternative is a promise of war and destruction, and the sorrowful end of humanity.

At this point, the foreign world leaders have some understandable questions.

"Before I declare martial law in New Deshret and upset a few million people, I must ask all of you a foolish old man question," the Pharikon of New Deshret says. "How does one account for all the *pegasei?*

Gwen replies that it's simple—*she* will locate the *pegasei* for everyone.

What follows is a global, SPC-sanctioned **international military operation**.

Multiple "initiated" individuals trained by Gwen to communicate with the *pegasei* are dispatched with military **special ops** enforcer teams to **liberate the *pegasei*** around the globe. The initiated will be able to "hear" the *pegasei* with their minds, no matter how remote or well hidden. And the troops will make sure there is compliance.

Linking of Minds: Gwen and Aeson

Will you join your mind with his through all of us?

The opportunity to **link minds** with each other is irresistible for **Gwen and Aeson**. When the pegasei make the offer to facilitate the process between them, naturally the couple who are soul mates take it, as described in **Survive**, Chapter 85.

> I feel another split-second explosion in my head.
> There's a secondary blast in the center of my
> forehead, and the tunnel widens to accommodate
> *another.*

Gwen and Aeson's experience of joining is profound, loving, and nearly indescribable.

There is a universe of emotion between them and their bond is deepened, but the joining comes to an abrupt end.

Apparently, the experience is simply too much for a human mind to handle. The mind connection can result in their **self-dissolution** as the two humans lose themselves in the other.

The *pegasei* have to regretfully terminate the link between Gwen and Aeson. Humanity has not evolved the **safety controls** necessary to put up **separation membranes** between their entity-selves.

Gwen and Aeson thank the *pegasei* for the experience, no matter how brief, knowing that the **spirit echoes** of their profound joining will remain with them permanently.

Pegasei Liberation

Gwen makes the brave promise to all the heads of state at the Imperial meeting that she can locate all the *pegasei*, even the hidden ones, all around the globe. Now she needs to make good on that promise (**Survive**, Chapter 86).

How to accomplish this at a distance? Turns out, the **frequency** itself is the connection between them. Once Gwen forms the note, the *pegasei* voices will respond to her call.

Arion demonstrates the beautiful trans-dimensional sequence that can only be "sung" by means of thought.

It occurs to me, this sound—it is forming a double helix inside my mind.

Like a DNA strand, this is a song of creation.

Arion tells her that once she sings, the *pegasei* will answer her at a distance—all of them.

Gwen conveys to the others the special double-helix sequence that will allow them to navigate to the locations of all the *pegasei* around the world.

The SPC-led pegasei *liberation project parameters:*

Step 1 – pass on the *pegasei* frequency to key individuals and establish a communication hierarchy. These same individuals will be leading special enforcer teams which are being selected specifically for this task from various Fleets around the globe.

Step 2 – announce to the public and prepare for pushback.

Step 3 – notify registered owners of *pegasei*, individuals and corporations, and issue confiscation warrants.

Step 4 – deploy enforcer teams.

Step 5 – start searching for illegal and hidden *pegasei* (that's where Gwen comes in, together with a handful of specially initiated others) in conjunction with international local authorities.

I ask Lady Irana very politely to stop and then explain to her my intent.

"My Imperial Lady, you want to release my *pegasus*?" she asks with wide eyes. "But why?"

> "No, I want *you* to release your *pegasus*
> yourself," I say. Then I sing the frequency and tell
> her to copy me.

As a typical *pegasei* "owner," with a doubtful expression, Lady Irana obeys Gwen. The moment she does so, she freezes in her tracks and stares at the little being imprisoned in the gilded cage, hovering at eye level before her and crying pitifully in her mind—Gwen can hear its frustration and discomfort echoing inside her head. And then Lady Irana begins to cry also. . . .

Moments later, the little *pegasus* soars into the sky, in a glorious explosion of mauve and orange light. Irana watches, holding open the cage door and smiling with serene wonder.

The *pegasus* cries joyfully and expresses gratitude.

And that's how it's done.

The operation proceeds around the globe. There are multiple raids of semi-legal *pegasei* "breeding" facilities, and they get visited by the **Pegasei Release Teams** or **PRTs**—consisting of one designated *pegasei* Communicator who knows the frequency, and special ops enforcer troops as military backup.

The quantum containment "faraday cage" fields are disabled. Harnesses and other means of containment are removed by reluctant *pegasei* handlers, even as PRT enforcement troops stand by, ready to interfere if needed.

And suddenly, clouds of plasma energy erupt from their bonds.

Once outside, the *pegasei* congregate in the open air to feel the full-spectrum warmth of Hel's light, feeding upon the energy of daylight. They gather together to form immense flocks in the lower atmosphere, hanging over cities like the aurora borealis.

Pegasei Retrieval Khenneb Mission

The last *pegasei* to be liberated are confined under strange circumstances in Khenneb, an ally nation located on the same Upper Continent. Khenneb specifically requests Gwen's help with a difficult retrieval of *pegasei* from an illegal subterranean facility inside mountain caves (**Survive**, Chapters 87-89).

Gwen is given a special ops PRT to assist her on the mission.

They fly in a large *ankhurat* ship to Khenneb, and once inside the hidden dimly-lit cave system, they find the strange sight of many orbs filled with captive *pegasei*.

But the **ancient spherical orbs** that contain these particular *pegasei* are unlike anything Gwen and the others have previously encountered.

The containment spheres are *intangible*, physically unreachable, **locked away in some other dimension.**

Apparently these pegasei have been trapped inside a **dimension threshold** for thousands of years—soon after the time of Landing— by some reckless ancient humans attempting to create another dimensional rift.

Gwen goes to work trying different things. She sings keying commands, but nothing works.

Meanwhile the PRT mission captain insists it's time to give up and go, since they are about to be overrun with local enemy soldiers.

Gwen gets a bright idea—to explode the **dimensional bubbles from the inside** using **light**!

The PRT operatives turn on their various light equipment, providing desperately needed nourishment to the starved *pegasei*.

The *pegasei* expand and rip apart their bonds, and are liberated.

Now all the *pegasei* are free to travel back along the wormhole into the rift on Earth.

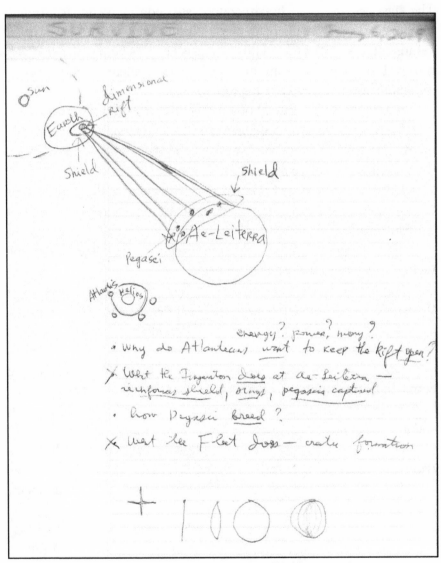

The Earth Rift and the Great Quantum Shield at Ae-Leiterra

The Pegasei Solution

Ultimately, the Imperator himself plays an important role in the *pegasei* solution to the problem of the ancient dimensional rift on Earth.

The *pegasei* have been liberated. But for some reason they are still around.

To understand why, the Imperator uses the frequency to connect with the *pegasei* directly. It is revealed that the *pegasei* were waiting for him.

Sacrifice. He had to make the personal choice at last. No one can make it for him. Even now, he is in turmoil regarding what must be done, what he has to do.

It's not enough that the *pegasei* must leave to properly close the rift. **They must also take something with them—***someone*.

Romhutat points at the **sarcophagus** of **Arlenari Kassiopei** and explains what must be done to fulfill destiny.

"She, this ancient female of my Dynasty, must be taken back to the Rim of Ae-Leiterra. There she must pass through the wormhole and into the rift on Earth—in effect, returning the *entangled quantum string* that is her essence—to be reunited with the remains of her twin brother Oron inside that rift. The powerful force of their entanglement,

stretched across the cosmic expanse, was keeping
it open all these eons, just as much as the *pegasei*.
Only then will the dimensional rift seal itself."

The Imperator himself must perform this time-critical task of delivering Arlenari to the wormhole.

The *pegasei* **cannot carry physical objects** of solid matter at a **speed** that **exceeds** physical parameters. It would take several months of fastest travel for the *pegasei* to carry her to the center of the Coral Reef Galaxy, to the Rim of Ae-Leiterra.

But it would take the Imperator only a few days, if he uses the Quantum Jump **without preliminary acceleration**—something only a highly trained Kassiopei with a Logos voice can do safely. And from there, the *pegasei* will take Arlenari inside the wormhole the rest of the way.

The Imperator departs on this mission while everyone else is deploying on theirs—the *astroctadra* **grand alignment mission** around the Helios system to combat the golden enemy light grid.

Gwen thinks that Arion left without saying goodbye, but the alien being is not gone yet. Gwen asks him/her/it to promise not to leave without a proper farewell.

There is never a proper farewell. But I promise not
to terminate our contact without your acceptance
of the precise ending of our time together.

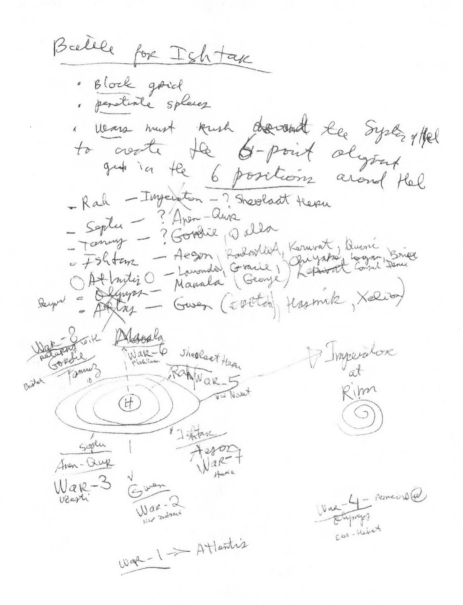

Final Battle for Ishtar and Rim Mission

Fast forward many critical events, with Gwen marooned in space. She gets the chance to see, via computer link in her space suit, the Imperator at the last stage of his one-way mission, on board his velo-cruiser. And she and Aeson get to speak with Romhutat Kassiopei for the last time.

The Imperator has only a few moments to say his final words of farewell to all.

"And now—we go to close the *bashtooh* rift on the other end of the universe! Can you see how bright it's gotten here? It's time to Jump! Ah—and now the *pegasei* are *singing!* Can you hear it, the frequency? All of the frequencies! *Sound must become light!*"

The Imperator is gone, but not all of the *pegasei*—not yet.

In the coming critical events, both Erita and Hasmik face **death in space**, but are mysteriously preserved and rescued by the *pegasei*, in their penultimate acts on behalf of humanity—as Arion explains.

It is time now. We must go and finish it. You have achieved Starlight, Gwen Lark who is Kassiopei. Strive not to forget it.

And if you do, remember—it is within reach but will **require constant effort to maintain comprehension** *of its trans-dimensional nature for a 3D-locked entity such as your species. To regain your understanding,* **look at the stars***, as Arlenari did, and it will return to you.*

Goodbye, Gwen Lark who is Kassiopei who wields Starlight. We leave your species now, to finish what we promised. And now—*They* are coming.

The rainbow plasma beings disappear.

Somewhere on Earth, in the middle of the Atlantic, the ancient dimensional rift has been **sealed**. The last of the *pegasei* pass through it, supposedly together with the mysterious Arlenari Kassiopei and the man who used to be the Imperator of Atlantis.

CHAPTER 16 – *Atlanteo* Language Glossary

Here's everything you wanted to know about *Atlanteo*, the primary Atlantean language of the colony planet, its linguistic origins, slang terms, general vocabulary, and more!

The following terms and expressions are used in the core series (**Qualify, Compete, Win, Survive**, and the novella **Aeson: Blue**). The sections below include popular Atlantean insults and curse words, Deshi Language terms, common Bay slang idioms, and Earth terms, and all the *Atlanteo* Language vocabulary to date.

Origins of *Atlanteo*

Atlantida is the word in the core language that means Atlantis. It is the original name of the Earth continent and of the colony planet, and also the first nation that was formed. The Greeks had retained the remnants of the Atlantean language in bits and pieces, and apparently passed it onward unto the ages. And now, ancient words and fragments are all that Earth has to remember the Atlanteans by, the once-great civilization that was Ancient Atlantis.

In many aspects, the Ancient Atlantean language is a predecessor to Earth's Ancient Greek, Ancient Egyptian, and possibly Mesopotamian, Sumerian, Urartu, and even Sanskrit. (The author used elements of all above, plus Armenian, Russian, Mandarin Chinese, and more, to create *Atlanteo*.)

Indeed, most ancient Earth languages carry in them remnants of *Atlanteo*. After all, Atlanteans ruled the ancient world—their culture and technology permeated all the Earth continents.

The Atlantean Perspective on Language

Modern Atlanteans studying contemporary Earth languages find them all rather beautiful—intricate, glorious, musical. On their way here, during the Earth Mission, many months are devoted to studying the various language families and groupings that Earth has produced since the last time Atlanteans were here, sharing the planet of origin. Meanwhile, back at home on Atlantis, most nations incentivize their general populations to study English and several other Earth languages in preparation for the refugees' arrival.

According to **Instructor Chior Kla** who teaches language on Gwen's ark-ship during their journey, most languages have common roots—like great trees and vines—and many of them entwine lovingly, mixing together to form new hybrids. At the time of Ancient Atlantis, their vibrant language was thriving and giving offshoots, which later became Earth's Ancient Egyptian and Ancient Greek, among others. Thus, when modern Earth teens begin to study the language of *Atlantida*, they will recognize many roots of words that they already know in their modern languages.

If you have studied a language other than your native language, then you already know what it's like to think in a different way about the same thing. Because that's all a new language is—a slightly *different* way of thinking and looking at the same world.

It's like putting on multi-colored sunglasses. It enriches a person's thought processes and blows up their imagination like a balloon. And it gives them the mysterious power to express themselves to others who normally might not be able to understand.

Now, I will tell you a secret. But first, I ask you this—what do you think is the *purpose* of language?

The most obvious purpose of language is it to communicate. It is also to share one's own life with other people. Language gives one the ability to become someone else.

But that's hardly all.

One secret aspect is that in the process of communicating, the speaker discards their own self and becomes a vessel for the *thing* that must be expressed—the meaning.

"The secret purpose of language is to *change everything*. And by everything I mean, your life, the life of others, the planet, the universe itself. Language is action, movement, life itself. It initiates progress, evolution. Language creates. If I recall correctly—in one of your ancient Earth holy books, there's the notion that 'in the beginning was the word.' I think it's a beautiful metaphor. Because if you think about it, the world itself is made up of metaphors—meaningful thought and image constructs."

Here is where *metaphors* and *similes* come into play. Similes and metaphors are figures of speech. They both let you describe and compare things by means of analogies. A simile uses comparison words "like" and "as," while a metaphor uses the imagery directly.

Synonyms are also involved. They are words that mean the exact same thing as other words.

"What if I told you that the word 'heart'—or *corazón, coeur, sertse, sin, seert, herz, hart, cuore, uummat, cridhe, kardia* or any other of the thousands of different language forms of the same thing we all have beating inside our chest cavity— is just a synonym? Because you can think of different languages as merely *vast groups of synonyms* of each other."

The more languages one learns, the more words one discovers to mean the same thing—which makes each thing that much more rich, powerful, wonderful! Suddenly that "thing" inside the chest—that *coeur, sertse,* heart—is no longer merely *one,* but *many.*

Knowing this, it's fun to begin learning the beautiful language of *Atlantida,* a proto-language for so many.

Fun Facts: Atlantean nouns have genders—male, female, and neuter. And some words have different meanings if they are *sung* as opposed to merely *spoken.*

Pronunciation

Ever wonder how to say all those names and terms? In general, the pronunciation is similar to Spanish or Italian, usually every letter is pronounced, and all the vowels are mostly short.

The vowels "a, e, i, o, u" are pronounced "ah," "eh," "ee," "oh," "ooh."

"a" as in "arbor"
"e" as in "elephant"
"i" as in "India"
"o" as in "onward"
"u" as in "oops"

For example, *"aeojir"* is pronounced "ah-eh-oh-JEER" with the stress falling on the last syllable (in caps).

Aeson's name has been simplified for the sake of the English-speaking Earth people to be pronounced like "Jason" without the "J." However, the true Atlantean pronunciation of his name is "Ah-eh-SOHN."

Xelio's name is pronounced "K-SEH-lee-oh" on Atlantis, while on Earth it has been simplified to "ZEH-lee-oh."

 For exciting real videos of Atlantean language tutorials, check out the **YouTube Channel!**
https://www.youtube.com/veranazarian-tag/

Atlantean Insults

Bakris – carrion, insult.

Bashtooh – common expletive, insult, comparable to d-word.

Chazuf – jerk, a-hole, generic crude term for guy primarily, can be an insult or affectionate.

Garooi – stupid, fool.

Hoohvak – idiot, fool (son of).

Fish-eater – generic insult, a show of disdain.

Maqooi **eater** – same as fish-eater.

Rawah bashtooh – "very much" *bashtooh*, an amplified version of *bashtooh*. Hot damn, or extra hard cursing.

Shar-ta-haak – buffoon, fool, stupid, idiot.

Shebet – crap (a piece of), junk.

Shibet – a person made of crap (son of, mother of).

Varqood – very strong expletive, an obscenity. Similar to f-word.

Varqoodat – very strong expletive, noun form of f-word, meaning a total mess.

Varqu – a strong expletive, noun form, referring to a person.

Deshi Language Words

Rahuqua – the ancient enemy aliens or "They," means "scourge."

Shiokuh nuuttos – good evening.

Idiom and Bay Slang

The following phrases are used by Kokayi Jeet and his mother, both Golden Bay natives speaking in strong idiom. Also heard on the streets of Themisera (Sky Tangle City), in Fish Town, and all around the Golden Bay.

- ***Bay Bean*** or simply ***bean*** – boy, guy, or male, sometimes means son.

- ***Bay Pebble*** or simply ***pebble*** – girl or female, sometimes means daughter.

- ***Hag*** – older woman, matron, sometimes means mother.

- ***Weather*** – mood, temper, attitude. Sample usage: "Don't you weather at me, Bay bean!" means "Don't have an attitude with me, boy." Sample two: "You take your weather out and show me your head," means "Stop your temper/show of attitude and tell me what's on your mind, or what you're thinking."

- ***Dropping gravity*** – caring, making time for something, thinking something is important. Sample usage: "You think I will drop gravity for this?" means "You think I care?"

- ***Morning in your head*** – understanding, sudden realization. Sample usage: "Ah, morning in your head?" means, "Ah, you understand now?"

"Luck and fortune, and steady winds, *amrevet*."

—Kokayi Jeet

Earth Terms and Slang

- *Goldilocks* – derogatory Earth slang for Atlanteans, to account for their habit of dying their hair gold.

- *Candy/Candies* – "short for Candidate," a term that originated in the RQC compounds during Qualification training.

- *Earthie* – the original slang term for Earth refugees, its usage proliferating during the journey in space, before the term *shìrén* became the dominant slang once they landed on Atlantis.

- *Shìrén* – Mandarin Chinese for "earthling," what Earth refugees call themselves on Atlantis, and what everyone on Atlantis calls them, since there are so many Earthie refugees who are Chinese-speaking.

Atlanteo Dictionary

The following *Atlanteo* language words appear in the core books of **The Atlantis Grail** series *(Qualify, Compete, Win, Survive)* and the novella *Aeson: Blue*, listed in alphabetical order:

A

Aeojir – tea, brewed from a plant similar to Earth's *camellia sinensis*, native to the colony plant Atlantis.

Agnios – fire. The *agnios* tree or "fire tree" is a native of Imperial *Atlantida*, found only along the Agnios Coast. It produces multi-colored resin, which becomes fossilized like amber, and is highly valued as a precious stone. "Pegasus Tears" is recently solidified gemstone, lighter in color. "Pegasus Blood" is ancient, darkened into deepest hues, considered most valuable. Plentiful during the early Colony period, it was over-harvested, and is very rare in present day Atlantis.

Akh, ba, ka – soul triumvirate, religious and spiritual terms for the three parts of the soul. The *akh* is the complete being reunited with all its soul parts in the afterlife. The *ba* is the individuality—the specific person, colored, tainted and shaped by the life experiences in the physical world. The *ka* is the immortal life force, the aspect that is divine.

Akhet – horizon. Also "Horizon Islands," when referring to the archipelago. The Akhet archipelago of seven small islands includes Benben Island (the largest, about three miles across) and serves as the site of the Game Zone of Stage Four of the Games.

Amre-ter – honorific address for father of spouse.

Amre-taq – honorific address for mother of spouse.

Amrevet-Ra – ancient Atlantean deity worshipped as Love in all its supreme aspects, and its priesthood cult, usually in charge of weddings and associated nuptial ceremonies. It encompasses all forms of love—platonic, erotic, familial, and all other varieties.

Amrevet – love, also the name of the largest moon of Atlantis, violet in color.

Amrevu – beloved. Aeson calls Gwen *"im amrevu"* or "my beloved."

Amreve – lover

Ankhurat – military fighter vessel, the biggest, heaviest fighter. One hundred personnel crew plus six Pilots, intended for boarding other vessels, with six heavy-caliber plasma guns and ten missiles. Nicknamed "Ankh, the Life Giver."

Archaeon Imperator – see Imperator.

Archaeona Imperatris – see Imperatris.

Ardukat – a military vessel: two-crew fighter, four guns, fine-focus burst and wide scatter-burst weapons capability, Pilot and Co-Pilot flight pair. The most common small combat ship in the Fleet.

Astra daimon – an informal brotherhood and sisterhood of the best pilots in the Star Pilot Corps. You cannot join, you may only be chosen. Literally means "star demon."

Astroctadra – a four-point star shape, in both two and three dimensions.

Atlantida – the Atlantean term for Atlantis, the planet, and for Imperial *Atlantida*, the nation.

B

Ba, ka, akh – soul triumvirate, religious and spiritual terms for the three parts of the soul. The *ba* is the individuality—the specific person, colored, tainted and shaped by the life experiences in the physical world. The *ka* is the immortal life force, the aspect that is divine. The *akh* is the complete being reunited with all its soul parts in the afterlife.

Bakris – carrion, insult.

Bakvi – two-pronged deep spoon, eating utensil. Can be used to stab food like a fork or pick up liquid like a spoon.

Bashtooh – common expletive, insult, comparable to d-word.

Bichugai – Atlantean variant of a lasso for roping animals.

C

Chazuf – jerk, a-hole, generic crude term for guy primarily, can be an insult or affectionate.

Chivkoor – soup ladle, an eating utensil similar to a spoon. Specifically, a bidirectional ladle utensil shaped like a boat, used to eat soup and dip in bowls. It has no handle, holds more than an Earth spoon, and you can sip or slurp the contents from either nose end of the "boat"—the prow or the stern. One end is slightly blunt and rounded, the other slightly pointy and angled.

Choonu – species of fish, harmless as adult, but when in small, baby larvae stage, similar to leeches, they eat anything that has blood. *Choonu* are one of the water hazards in Stage Three of the Games.

Chuvuat – thank you.

D

Dea – day

Delphit – dolphin, originally brought from Earth to Atlantis and allowed to evolve in the new environment.

Depet – boat, ship, generic term for space vessel.

Depet-Ra – a vessel that becomes the Command Vessel once it is boarded by the Fleet Commander. For example, when a battle barge carries the SPC Fleet Commander it gets the temporary designation of *Depet-Ra* (similar to Air Force One, the airplane of the US President on Earth). Once the Commander departs, that battle barge is again simply called a War.

Deshi – the language of New Deshret.

E

Ellaemai – sing (imperative command)

Ellaetris – singer female

Ellaetor – singer male

Ellam – song (noun)

Ellae – to sing (infinitive)

Eos – morning

Eos **bread** – breakfast

Eos **pie** – a kind of hand pie, usually fruit-filled.

Eoseiara – a traditional wedding song on Atlantis, sang by the bride and bridegroom during the ceremony. The word *Eoseiara* means "the dawning," "dawn-like," or "that which is of the dawn," and implies a new beginning.

F

Fuchmik – a dry, barely sweet, dessert stick made with nuts and dried fruit, originating in the city of Khur in Shuria.

G

Garooi – stupid, fool.

Gebi – earthling, something that came from Earth, in Classical *Atlanteo*.

H

Hereret – a hereditary ruler of a lesser nation, similar to a "duke," usually supported in governing by a council. Not an absolute power holder. The *Crown Hereret* in Vai Naat is a hereditary royal similar to a "duke," and granted primary "Crown" powers by a family vote from a pool of other regional Hererets.

Hermei (singular) / *Hermeitar* (plural) – an Atlantean measure of length, equivalent to about a meter or three feet.

Hetep-nete – goodbye

Hetmet – a hereditary ruler of a lesser nation, smaller than a "king," usually supported in governing by a council. Not an absolute power holder.

Hoohvak – idiot, fool (son of).

Hurucaz – small, grape-like fruit

I

Ihamar – an airy, frozen fruit delight similar to ice cream, a dessert.

Imperator – monarch sovereign ruler of Imperial *Atlantida*. Full title: *Archaeon Imperator*.

Imperatris – female monarch sovereign ruler of Imperial *Atlantida*, or consort spouse of the reigning *Imperator*. Full title: *Archaeona Imperatris*.

Impero – (adjective) Imperial.

Im-seki – self-murder, suicide, considered to be an act of great dishonor.

Im – my, as in *"im amrevu,"* or "my beloved."

Im sen-i-senet, astra daimon – "my brothers and sisters, star demons"

Irephuru – traditional wedding circle dance, based on concentric circles—like the original city of Poseidon on Ancient Atlantis on Earth. The Newlyweds step into the center of the dance floor and perform intricate dance figures, circling each other, touching hands and briefly embracing for no more than three heartbeats, and not breaking eye contact for more than three heartbeats. Others join the dance by forming a second circle of four people around the couple.

The third circle has eight people, the next sixteen, the next circle can be as large as people want. Circles spin in opposite directions, holding and releasing hands. The objective for the central couple is to escape outward and get out of the circle by swapping with a random person in the next circle. Moving from circle to circle while avoiding being pulled back in, they exit the dance.

Iret (singular) – see *Iretar*.

Iretar (plural) – Imperial *Atlantida* national currency, money. *Iret* (singular) is a single coin. Available as metal coins, roll-up scroll bills, and digital versions. Conversion rate with Earth currency has not been determined, and it is not really comparable to the British pound sterling, Australian dollar, Canadian dollar, or the Euro. In general, it converts much higher in value than a US dollar.

Irt – a species of antelope, herd animal.

J

Jeleleo – a traditional New Year's Day dessert, similar to *eos* pie but family sized, which must be eaten only during the 30-daydream period of Midnight Ghost Time on New Year's Day but before the final heartbeat of the day, Null Hour. Any leftovers must be taken outside.

K

Ka, ba, akh – soul triumvirate, religious and spiritual terms for the three parts of the soul. The *ka* is the immortal life force, the aspect that is divine. The *ba* is the individuality—the specific person, colored, tainted and shaped by the life experiences in the physical world. The *akh* is the complete being reunited with all its soul parts in the afterlife.

Kassiopeion – temple of the Kassiopei cult of divinity. The temple building is located on the Imperial Palace complex premises, and is one of the tallest structures on these grounds. It is long and rectangular, with one narrow end incorporating a raised section with elements of a ziggurat tower and a flat-top pyramid.

Kefarai – freshman (plural, singular, collective, masculine, feminine) slang for First Year student such as Fleet Cadet.

Kemetareon – the great square Imperial Kemet Forum, a part of an ultra-modern convention center-like complex of several stadiums, theaters, exhibit halls, and connecting buildings, located in downtown Poseidon.

Khepri – military fighter vessel, a four-Pilot team fighter, with four guns like the *ardukat*, but uses heavy-caliber artillery, able to eject plasma at a higher density from multiple thick nozzles in each gun. Additionally equipped with four guided missiles and armed probes. Serves as an attack bomber for major targets.

Kipt – drink stirring stick, eating implement.

Kopurai – a variety of wood.

Kuri – plant harvested for fabrics and textiles.

Kwugu – a common bean, eaten by humans and animals. Can be dried and stored for later consumption.

L

Lawu – a deep brown ale.

Lvikao – an Atlantean caffeinated hot drink similar to both coffee and cocoa, with complex spices and the aroma of a pastry shop.

M

Mafdet – solo fighter military vessel, the lightest, smallest, fastest, most agile, intended for air-to-air combat. Nicknamed the "Needle of Justice." Only the most experienced Pilots are permitted to fly.

Mag-heitar – measure of distance similar to ten kilometers.

Mamai – mother

Maqooi – a type of fish and its eggs, the Atlantean version of caviar.

Maqooi **eater** – insult, implying a fish eater.

Mar-Yan – the Rider; the third month of each season on the Atlantean Calendar; one of the moons of Atlantis.

Medoi – a kind of fruit, common filling in a fruit-filled *eos* pie.

Mei-Mamai – grandmother

Mei-Papai – grandfather

N

Nebetareon – a round mid-size stadium building topped by a geodesic dome roof, located in downtown Poseidon. The *Nebetareon* is part of an ultra-modern convention center-like complex of several stadiums, theaters, exhibit halls, and connecting buildings. This is the location of Gwen's interview on Tiago's show.
Nefero – beautiful
Nefero eos – good morning.
Nefero dea – good afternoon.
Nefero niktos – good evening, good night.
Nefir / nefira – beauty (person, male / female).
Nikkari – a fruit that is commonly used as a juice, producing "a thick algae-greenish liquid that tastes like watermelon ambrosia." Gwen's favorite Atlantean drink.
Niktos – night, evening.
Nomarch – position of authority over space station or small region on the planet surface.
Noohd – lip color, lipstick, lip gloss.

O

Orahemai – dance (imperative command)
Orahetris – dancer, female
Orahetor – dancer, male
Orakh – dance (noun)
Orahe – to dance (infinitive)
Oratorat – elected position of government leadership, specific to Eos-Heket, comparable to prime minister or president.

P

Palatean – stone
Papai – father

Pegasei – quantum trans-dimensional aliens introduced in the main series.

Pegasus – singular form of *pegasei*. The original concept of the Ancient Greek flying horse, the Pegasus, evolved from the composite images of ordinary horses and birds that the *pegasei* gleaned from human minds and compiled into the imaginary animal shape that later became mythic. Also, the second month of each season on the Atlantean Calendar, and one of the moons of Atlantis.

Pharikon – title of the sovereign ruler of New Deshret, equivalent to the *Imperator* of Imperial *Atlantida*. Generic ancient term for ruler, king, emperor, sovereign. On Earth this original *Atlanteo* term was borrowed and used in Ancient Egypt, evolving into the much later title "Pharaoh."

Pharikone – royal (adjective), king-like.

Pharikoneon – the Imperial Throne Hall, the most ancient, grand, formal chamber in the Imperial Palace where the biggest Court Assemblies and ceremonies are held. It contains the original Imperial Thrones and Seats.

Phoinios – purple in Ancient Greek. *Phoinios* Heights, or "Purple Heights" is the name of the region in the City of Poseidon where Aeson owned his personal estate, his preferred home away from the Imperial Palace.

Puzuk – butt, behind, rear end.

Q

R

Rai – a hereditary ruler of a lesser nation, the equivalent of "king," usually supported in governing by a council. Not an absolute power holder.

Rawah bashtooh – "very much" *bashtooh*, an amplified version of *bashtooh*. Hot damn, or extra hard cursing.

Re-re-xut – an imaginary insect that is attracted to the sound of human snoring (also called the *snorat* bug in the main series).

Ruiv – black-veined stone.

S

Saa – child
Saai – children
Saret – wisdom
Saret-i-xerera – exclamation and verbal salute, translates as "wisdom and glory."
Scolariat – class
Sitahrra – an ancient traditional stringed musical instrument with elements reminiscent of a lute, lyre, harp, zither and even the guitar. It has a hollow wooden resonant body (usually with a round "hoop" or medallion exterior frame encircling an *astroctadra*-shaped resonance chamber—or the reverse, an *astroctadra*-shaped body with a spherical resonance chamber), a long neck, and strings made of various materials including metal.
Sebasaret – a large midrange military transport, not considered a fighter. A command ship carrier for ranking officers, military personnel, and other vessels. Can be used as transport and command center, and for science research in addition to military deployment. Has weapons capability, but no guns, only guided missiles. Different combinations of lesser fighter ships can fit inside.
Sebeku – crocodile, originally brought from Earth to Atlantis and allowed to evolve in the new environment.
Sen – brother
Sen-i-senet – brothers and sisters
Senef sedjet – really big orange cats, evolved from Earth tigers or jaguars.
Senet – sister
Sesemet – Atlantean horse.
Sha – generic term for an animal that is a predator. Dangerous animals thought to be the creations of the old darkness god.
Shar-ta-haak – buffoon, fool, stupid, idiot.
Shebet – crap (a piece of), junk.
Shibet – a person made of crap (son of, mother of).

Shuut – (Feather/Tail) a unique Fleet rear formation which consists of specialized ships, usually carrying civilian VIPs and wartime correspondents, that are capable of escape at a moment's notice. The *Shuut* can also perform other non-standard tasks on behalf of the Fleet during battle.

Snorat – not an actual Atlantean word but a silly term made up by Oalla to mockingly refer to the *re-re-xut*, an imaginary "snoring bug."

Stadion – stadium, also proper name of the biggest stadium in the Atlantis Grail complex, officially known as The Atlantis Grail Stadium. It houses the immense Atlantis Grail Monument and serves as the permanent site of the Stage One Game Zone of the Games, and the formal Commencement and Closing Ceremonies and other grand spectacles.

T

Taq – madam (polite address)

Ter – sir (mister, polite address)

Ter-i-taq – gentlemen and ladies, a general respectful group address.

Tif-nu-sha – a water *sha*, a shark, originally brought from Earth to Atlantis and allowed to evolve in the new environment. *Tif-nu-sha* are one of the water hazards in Stage Three of the Games.

U

Uas-ames-ga-uas – full name of weapon commonly abbreviated as *uas-uas*; see below.

Uas-uas – hand-to-hand combat weapon, a short pair of club sticks attached with a cord, resembling Earth *nunchaku* or nunchucks.

Uraeus – headdress and gold insignia band in the form of a serpent ready to strike worn by the Imperator. Greater and Lesser forms exist. Lesser form is coiled serpent at rest worn by the Imperial Crown Prince.

V

Varqood – very strong expletive, an obscenity. Similar to f-word.

Varqoodat – very strong expletive, noun form of f-word, meaning a total mess.
Varqu – a strong expletive, noun form, referring to a person.
Vati – aides (plural of aide).
Viatoios – orichalcum-based alloy, bullet-proof, blade-proof, and fire-proof silvery fabric material used for fine body armor and other protective gear, worn by Gwen in the Games.
Vuchusei – sweet, tasty, pleasurable, soulful, can be used as a sensual term in the erotic sense.

W

Wedjat – the Kassiopei eye, genetic, with a fine dark outline around the eyelids, a kind of natural eyeliner.
Wixameret – welcome

X

Xerera – glory
Xolapei – vitriol, sulfuric acid, water diluted and one of the water hazards in Stage Three of the Games.

Y

Yatet – a species of antelope, herd animal.

Z

ATLANTIS
(ATLANTIDA)
LOWER HEMISPHERE

TheAtlantisGrail.com

TAG Con and Fan Resources Online

In 2020 the wonderful fandom of *The Atlantis Grail* held the first virtual TAG Fan Convention. **TAG Con 2020 Virtual Intergalactic** was a blast!

So much fun was had by all that it was decided to continue this tradition every year, with **TAG Con 2021 Quantum Blue**, and **TAG Con 2022 Eos Exodus**.

 TAG Con – visit the **convention website** and join the fun!
http://tag.fan/tagcon.htm

The virtual international convention is now in its third year, and there is an in-person version being planned, pending on world events. Meanwhile, various regional in-person meetups are being scheduled on the official **TAG Fan Discussion Forum.**

All past convention events and panels are available to be viewed on YouTube.

Have questions?

Visit the **TAG DOT FAN** website!

The following TAG-related websites and links are very useful for the dedicated TAG fan:

 Official **author** website:
http://www.veranazarian.com/

Get on my **Insider Mailing List!**
http://eepurl.com/hKaeo

 TAG Fandom website:
http://www.tag.fan

TAG **official website**:
http://www.theatlantisgrail.com/

Frequently Asked Questions **(FAQ)**:
http://www.theatlantisgrail.com/#faq

The Atlantis Grail **Fan Discussion Forum**:
http://atlantisgrail.proboards.com/

 Astra Daimon and Shoelace Girls (Facebook fan group):
https://www.facebook.com/groups/adasg/

The Atlantis Grail – SPOILERS (Facebook fan group):
https://www.facebook.com/groups/tag2spoilers/

 Facebook TAG Page:
https://www.facebook.com/AtlantisGrail/

Color Quadrant **Quiz**:
http://www.norilana.com/TAG-Quiz.htm

 Atlantean **Calendar Date Converter**:
http://tag.fan/TAG-Calendar.html

YouTube Channel:
https://www.youtube.com/veranazarian-tag/

TAG Con – **Fandom Convention**
http://tag.fan/tagcon.htm

TAG Music Pinterest board:
https://www.pinterest.com/veranazarian/music-of-the-atlantis-grail/

 TAG **Wiki**:

https://theatlantisgrail.fandom.com/wiki/The_Atlantis_Grail_Wiki

Linktree (**every link** in one place!)
https://linktr.ee/VeraNazarian

If You Enjoyed Exploring
THE ATLANTIS GRAIL COMPANION
You are a Superfan!

Want to start the journey from the beginning?
*Catch up with your **free** copy of **QUALIFY**,*
*book one of **The Atlantis Grail**!*

*More **TAG novellas** and **novels** coming soon,*
including the 5th full-length TAG novel!

*But first—a new **prequel series** exploring the events*
of Ancient Atlantis, 12,500 years ago, begins in:

EOS (Dawn of the Atlantis Grail, Book One)
Coming soon!

While you wait, for a change of pace, try the intensely romantic historical epic fantasy **Cobweb Bride** or the madly hilarious **Vampires are from Venus, Werewolves are from Mars**.

Don't miss another book by Vera Nazarian!

Subscribe to the *mailing list* to be notified when the next books by Vera Nazarian are available. We promise not to spam you or chit-chat, only make occasional book release and news announcements. http://eepurl.com/hKaeo

Want to talk about it with other fans? Join the fun at **The Atlantis Grail Fan Discussion Forum**

About the Author

Vera Nazarian is a two-time Nebula Award® Finalist, a Dragon Award 2018 Finalist, and a member of Science Fiction and Fantasy Writers of America. As a double refugee, after emigrating from the USSR during the Cold War, and then escaping from the Civil War in Lebanon (by way of Greece), she immigrated to the USA as a kid, sold her first story at 17, and has been published in numerous anthologies and magazines, honorably mentioned in Year's Best volumes, and translated into eight languages.

Vera made her novelist debut with the critically acclaimed *Dreams of the Compass Rose,* followed by *Lords of Rainbow.* Her novella *The Clock King and the Queen of the Hourglass* made the 2005 Locus Recommended Reading List. Her debut collection *Salt of the Air* contains the 2007 Nebula Award-nominated "The Story of Love." Recent work includes the 2008 Nebula Finalist novella *The Duke in His Castle,* science fiction collection *After the Sundial* (2010), *The Perpetual Calendar of Inspiration* (2010), three Jane Austen parodies, *Mansfield Park and Mummies* (2009), *Northanger Abbey and Angels and Dragons* (2010), and *Pride and Platypus: Mr. Darcy's Dreadful Secret* (2012), all part of her *Supernatural Jane Austen Series*, a parody of self-help and supernatural relationships advice, *Vampires are from Venus, Werewolves are from Mars: A Comprehensive Guide to Attracting Supernatural Love* (2012), *Cobweb Bride Trilogy* (2013), and the four books in the bestselling international cross-genre phenomenon series *The Atlantis Grail,* now optioned for development as a feature film and/or TV series, *Qualify* (2014), *Compete* (2015), *Win* (2017), and *Survive* (2020).

After many years in Los Angeles, Vera now lives in a small town in Vermont. She uses her Armenian sense of humor and her Russian sense of suffering to bake conflicted pirozhki and make art.

In addition to being a writer, philosopher, and award-winning artist, she is also the publisher of Norilana Books.

 Official website: http://www.veranazarian.com/

Get on my **Mailing List!**
http://eepurl.com/hKaeo

The Atlantis Grail Fan Discussion Forum:
http://atlantisgrail.proboards.com/

 Astra Daimon and Shoelace Girls (Facebook fan group):
https://www.facebook.com/groups/adasg/

The Atlantis Grail – SPOILERS (Facebook fan group):
https://www.facebook.com/groups/tag2spoilers/

 TAG official website:
http://www.theatlantisgrail.com/

TAG Fandom website:
http://www.tag.fan

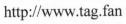 **Norilana Books**:
http://www.norilana.com/

Twitter:
http://twitter.com/Norilana

 Facebook Author Page:
http://www.facebook.com/VeraNazarian/

Facebook TAG Page:
https://www.facebook.com/AtlantisGrail/

Instagram:
https://www.instagram.com/vera_nazarian/

 YouTube Channel:
https://www.youtube.com/veranazarian-tag/

TikTok:
https://www.tiktok.com/@veranazarian

 Goodreads:

http://www.goodreads.com/author/show/186145.Vera_Nazarian

LibraryThing:
http://www.librarything.com/author/nazarianvera

 Wattpad:
http://www.wattpad.com/user/VeraNazarian

Linktree
https://linktr.ee/VeraNazarian

Blogs:
http://www.inspiredus.com/
http://urbangirlvermont.blogspot.com/
http://norilana.livejournal.com/

Acknowledgements

There are so many of you whose unwavering, loving support helped me bring this book to life. My gratitude is boundless, and I thank you with all my heart (and in alphabetical order, because in any other way lies madness)!

First, my immense gratitude to the incredible *astra daimon* and superfan Nancy Huett, who compiled a comprehensive list of every edible item mentioned in the books, plus cross checked numerous other facts and stats. Same goes for Liz Logotheti whose tremendous facts-and-figures and number crunching skills are the basis for the Atlantean Calendar Date Converter web tool, and whose fabulous fan art is the gold standard as far as the author is concerned.

To my absolutely brilliant first readers, advisors, topic experts, editors, proofreaders, fandom moderators, TAG Con Committee members and friends, Ricki Bristow, Elizabeth Logotheti, Heather Dryer, Jeanne Miller, Nancy Huett, Nydia Fernandez Burdick, Roby James, Shelley Bruce, Susan Franzblau, Teri N. Sears, Mary C. Sellar, Kerry Vosswinkel, and West Yarbrough McDonough.

To the lovely and wonderful group of Vermont writers and friends, Anne Stuart, Ellen Jareckie, Lina Gimble, and Valerie Gillen, and to my dear friends in more distant places, Lisa Silverthorne and Patricia Duffy Novak.

To all the wonderful and enthusiastic members of the "Astra Daimon and Shoelace Girls" Facebook group, "The Atlantis Grail – SPOILERS" Facebook group, and the official TAG Discussion Forum on ProBoards.

To my awesome and fabulous Wattpad friends and fans who keep re-reading each TAG preview chapter and making me smile, laugh, and otherwise delight in your hilarious, stunning, amazing, and insightful responses to the story! Thank you immensely!

If I've forgotten or missed anyone, the fault is mine; please know that I love and appreciate you all.

Finally, I would like to thank all of you dear reader friends, who decided to take my hand and step into my world of **The Atlantis Grail**.

My deepest thanks to all for your support!

Before you go, you are kindly invited to leave a **review of this book!**

Reviews are a wonderful way to help the author! They are also an exciting opportunity to share your honest thoughts with other readers, so **please post yours**, in as many places as possible!

CPSIA information can be obtained
at www.ICGtesting.com
Printed in the USA
LVHW040421110122
708163LV00001B/33